# 旅館英語

# Practical Hotel
# English

Andrew W. Peat ◎ 著

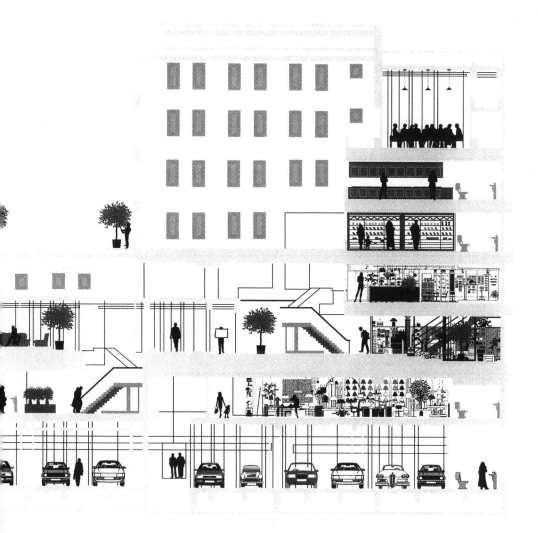

## 獻 詞

　　僅將本書獻給我最親愛的太太Maria以及二個女兒Natasha與Isabel；她們讓我的人生充滿了喜悅。同時也感謝我的母親在校對上的協助以及我的助理教師Eva為本書的翻譯與發音所做的努力。


*Andrew W. Peat*

# Introduction

This text is specifically designed to train workers in the hotel, restaurant and service industries to speak polite, courteous, on-the-job English. This text can be used by both service training schools and in-house hotel training programs. Specific examples are given with exercises following which can easily be adapted to different hotel and restaurant properties' situations.

A common mistake made in Asian English training programs is that the native language is used to teach English. This is like learning how to drive a car by riding a bicycle. The results will tend to be quite poor. Our text, following international practice and the pattern of our previous 2 Travel English books (Tourism English 1, 2), focuses almost exclusively on teaching English by using English

To simplify the learning experience and create a generic hotel atmosphere, this book will revolve around a standard, international-class 4 star hotel called the Chinese Hotel, complete with coffee shop, Western and Chinese restaurants, and a bar. The types of rooms are: standard, deluxe, suite, and Presidential Suite. Generally, in the various conversations and exercises, hotel employees will be designated "A", guests will be "B", and multiple guests "C", "D", and so on.

Simple and polite English forms are used throughout to enable learners to learn appropriate and courteous English quickly. An abundance of various exercises will also help improve the rate at which students learn basic hotel English.

# Contents

# Part III : Housekeeping

# Part V : Hotel Management

# *Part I : The Front Desk*

# Unit 1

# Room Reservations

## Dialogs

### 1. Making a Reservation

*B: The guest, Tim Beckett, calls the hotel and wants to book a standard room for May 10-14.*

*A: Hotel employee (Staff): Answers the phone and accepts the reservation.*

A: Reservations. May I help you?

B: Yes. I'd like to book a room.

A: Yes, sir. For which date would you like a reservation?

B: I will arrive on May 10th and leave the morning of the 14th.

A: Yes, sir. How many guests will there be in your party?

B: Just myself.

A: Would you like a standard room or a deluxe room?

B: What are the prices?

A: Standard rooms are NT$2500 and deluxe rooms are NT$3000, and there is a 15% service charge.

B: I'll take a standard.

A: Yes, sir. Please hold for a moment while I check our bookings. All right, sir, we can book you into a standard room for the dates you requested. May I have your name, please?

B: Tim Beckett.

A: Could you please spell your surname, Mr. Beckett?

B: B.E.C.K.E.T.T.

A: Thank you. One standard room for Mr. Beckett at NT$2500 per night for 4 nights from May 10th through the 13th, departing on the 14th.

B: That's right.  Thank you.

A: Thank you, sir.  We look forward to seeing you.

## Vocabulary

1. **book** [bʊk]  v.訂— to engage ahead of time; to reserve

   *I want to book an airplane ticket to Hong Kong on Thursday morning.*

2. **reservation** [rɛzəˋveʃən] n.預訂— arrangement to keep something for someone.

   *My travel agent has made all the reservations for my journey.*

3. **party** [ˋpartɪ] n.派對— gathering of persons; a group of people

   *There will be a party of 20 guests coming at 7:00.*

4. **standard** [ˋstændəd] adj.標準的— common; average

   *10 dollars is the standard price for this kind of book.*

5. **deluxe** [dɪˋlʌks] adj.豪華的— notably luxurious or elegant; not standard

   *Only rich people can eat at this deluxe restaurant.*

6. **surname** [ˈsɜˌnem] n.姓— that part of a person's name that is common to all members of the family; the family name; last name

*Smith is a very common English surname.*

# Dialogs

## 2. Making Group Reservations

*B: Martha Wiles, a company secretary, is calling to make a reservation for a group from her company.*

A: Reservations. May I help you?

B: Yes. This is Martha Wiles, secretary for the Harris Corporation. We'll be having a group of managers and engineers visit from September 4th to the 8th. We'd like to book 7 rooms with twin beds. Do you offer meal programs or group discounts?

A: Just a moment please while I check reservations. (Checks computer.) Yes, ma'am, we can confirm 7 rooms for September 4th to the 8th. Did you say this is for the Harris Corporation?

B: Yes, that's right.

A: Ms. Wiles, about meal programs, we offer coupons for a Continental Breakfast for NT$120 per guest or an American Buffet Breakfast at NT$250 per guest. As a group, you qualify for a 15% discount on rooms.

B: That's fine.

A: Do you wish to order breakfast coupons? The coupons will be handed over at check-in.

B: Yes.There will be a total of 11 people. Give us the Buffet Breakfast.

A: 11 for Buffet. Will your group be arriving by international flight?

B: Yes. RBA flight 057, which should arrive at 4 p.m.

A: Thank you. This way we can hold the rooms in case of late arrival.

B: Do you have small or medium sized conference rooms available?

A: We have several conference rooms and halls. If you'll hold for just a moment, I can transfer you to the manager in charge.

B: Yes, please.

## Vocabulary

1. **secretary** [ˈsɛkrəˌtɛrɪ] n.秘書— an employee (often a woman) who deals with office communications

   *In this company we have 3 secretaries to answer phones and do typing.*

2. **manager** [ˈmænɪdʒɚ] n.負責人— person who controls the daily work of a business

   *If you have a problem, you can talk to our manager.*

3. **engineer** [ɛndʒəˋnɪr] n.工程師— person who works with engines, machines, or designing equipment

*His father is a motorcycle engineer.*

4. **offer** [ˋɔfɚ] v.給予— hold out; put forward to be accepted or refused; give

*We can offer you a special price of 2 rooms for NT$4000.*

5. **discount** [ˋdɪskaʊnt] n.折扣— amount of money which may be taken off the full price; a special price

*We give a 10% discount for payment by cash.*

6. **confirm** [kənˋfɝm] v.證實— to make plans stronger; to repeat or remind of plans

*Please confirm your reservation by sending us NT$2000.*

7. **coupon** [ˋkupan] n.折價券— ticket which gives the holder the right to receive something

*With this coupon, you can get a 20% discount.*

8. **continental breakfast** [kɑntəˋnɛntḷ] [ˋbrɛkfəst] n.歐式早餐— a light, first meal, usually coffee or tea and bread

*The NT$2500 room charge includes a continental breakfast.*

9. **buffet** [bʌfɪt] n.自助餐— informal meal where guests choose food from a table instead of being served by a

waitress at their table

*Tonight we are offering a special buffet dinner for only NT$300.*

10. **qualify** [ˈkwaləfaɪ] v.限制— to become entitled to; to be able to receive or do

    *She is qualified to teach English.*

11. **in case of** [ɪn] [kes] [ɑv] 如果發生— in the event of; if... then

    *In case of fire, ring the bell and leave the building.*

12. **conference** [ˈkɑnfərəns] n.會議— meeting for discussions; exchange of views

    *We have had many international conferences held in our hotel.*

13. **transfer** [trænsˈfɝ] v.轉換— change position; move from one place to another

    *Next month, I will be tranferred from the Western Restaurant to the Coffee Shop.*

# Dialogs

## 3. Confirming a Reservation

> **B: The guest, Larry Armour, wishes to confirm his reservation for a standard room for December 3-7.**

A: Reservations. May I help you?

B: Yes. I'm calling to confirm my reservation.

A: Yes, sir. May I have your name, please?

B: Yes. My name is Larry Armour.

A: Could you spell your surname, please?

B: Armour. A.R.M.O.U.R.

A: May I have the date of your reservation, Mr. Armour?

B: December 3rd to 7th.

A: Just a moment, please.... Mr. Armour?

B: Yes.

A: We have you confirmed in a standard room from

December 3rd to 7th.  Thank you for confirming your reservation.

B: Thank you.  Goodbye.

## Dialogs

### 4. Canceling a Reservation

> **B: The guest, June Taylor, wishes to cancel her reservation for a deluxe room, July 7-9.**

A: Reservations. May I help you?

B: Yes, I would like to cancel my reservation.

A: May I have your name, ma'am?

B: June Taylor.

A: Could you spell your surname, please?

B: Yes.  T.A.Y.L.O.R.

A: Thank you. Just a moment, please.... Ms. Taylor?

B: Yes.

A: We have cancelled your reservation for July 7th to 9th. Would you like to make a reservation for another date, ma'am?

B: No, thank you.

A: Ms. Taylor, because you had a guaranteed reservation, there is a NT$1000 cancellation charge.

B: Well, I don't understand. I'm giving you plenty of time. I'm sure you can find someone else to use the room.

A: I'm sorry, Ms. Taylor, but this is a rule for all guaranteed reservations.

B: But it doesn't make sense. You don't have to charge me if you can find someone else to take the room!

A: If you would like, you may talk with the assistant manager.

B: Well, all right, I'll talk with the assistant manager.

A: Just a moment, Ms. Taylor, and I'll transfer the call.

## Vocabulary

1. **cancel** [ˈkænsl̩] v.刪掉— say that something already arranged will not be done

   *We decided to cancel the order for new televisions, because we don't need them.*

2. **suite** [swit] n.套房— a set of rooms; several rooms connected in a hotel

   *Our hotel offers two kinds of suites, standard and deluxe.*

3. **guarantee** [gærənˈti] v.保證— promise; to make certain

   *Our hotel wants to guarantee our guests' happiness.*

**Exercises** ——————————————

## ▸▸ *I. Complete the Dialogs* ◂◂

### 1. Making a Reservation

> *B: Guest: Name is Bill Davis. Wants to book a standard room for March 5-7.*
> *A: Hotel employee: Answer the phone and accept the reservation.*

A: Reservations. _____?

B: Yes. I'd like to book a room.

A: Yes, sir. _____?

B: I will arrive on March 5th and leave the morning of the 8th.

A: Yes, sir. How many _____?

B: Just myself.

A: _____?

B: What are the prices?

A: _____?

B: I'll take a standard.

A: Yes, sir.  Please hold _____.

   All right, sir, _____.

   May I _____?

B: Bill Davis.

A: _____?

B: D.A.V.I.S.

A: _____.

B: That's right.  Thank you.

A: Thank you, sir.  We look forward to seeing you.

## 2. Making Group Reservations

*B: Sanya Freole, a company secretary, is calling to make a reservation for a group from her company.*

A: Reservations. _____?

B: Yes. This is Sanya Freole, secretary for the Queens Corporation. We'll be having a group of managers and engineers visit from October 8th to the 12th. We'd like to book 6 rooms with twin beds. Do you offer meal programs or group discounts?

A: Just a moment please. (Checks computer.)

Yes, ma'am, we can _____. Did you say this is for the Queens Corporation?

B: Yes, that's right.

A: Ms. Freole, about meal programs, _____.

As a group.

B: That's fine.

A: Do you wish to order breakfast coupons? _____

_____.

B: Yes. There will be a total of 10 people. Give us the Buffet Breakfast.

A: 10 for Buffet. Will_____flight?

B: Yes. KNA flight 034, which should arrive at 2 p.m.

A: Thank you. This way _____.

B: Do you have small or medium sized conference rooms

available?

A: Yes, ma'am.  If you'll hold for just a moment, _____

_____.

B: Yes,  please.

## 3. Confirming a Reservation

> **B: Guest:  Name is Lawrence Waters. Wishes to confirm his reservation for a standard room for August 13-16.**

A: Reservations. _____?

B: Yes.  I'm calling to confirm my reservation.

A: Yes, sir. _____?

B: Yes.  My name is Lawrence Waters.

A: _____?

B: Waters. W.A.T.E.R.S.

A: _____?

B: August 13th to 16th.

A: Just a moment, please....  Mr. Waters?

B: Yes.

A: _____.

B: Thank you. Goodbye.

## 4. Canceling a Reservation

> **B: Guest: Name is Betty Sanders. Wishes to cancel her**
> **reservation for a deluxe room, November 7-9.**

A: Reservations. _____?

B: Yes, I would like to cancel my reservation.

A: _____?

B: Betty Sanders.

A: _____?

B: Yes. Sanders. S.A.N.D.E.R.S.

A: Thank you. _____?

B: Yes.

A: We have cancelled _____

_____?

B: No. thank you.

A: Ms. Sanders, because _____

_____.

B: Well, I don't understand. I'm giving you plenty of time. I'm sure you can find someone else to use the room.

A: I'm sorry, Ms. Sanders, _____.

B: But it doesn't make sense. You don't have to charge me if you can find someone else to take the room!

A: If you would like, _____.

B: Well, all right, I'll talk with the assistant manager.

A: Just a moment, Ms. Taylor, _____.

# Unit 2

# The Doorman and Bellboy

**Dialogs**

## 1. Receiving Guests

*A taxi pulls up in front of the Chinese Hotel. The doorman goes forward to open the car door and help the guests out.*

A: Good afternoon, sir.  Good afternoon, ma'am. Welcome to the Chinese Hotel.

B: Thank you.

A: Are you checking in?

B: Yes, we are.

A: Do you have luggage?

B: In the trunk.

A: Yes, sir. If you go in the door, you'll find the reception desk on your left. I'll have your luggage brought over for you. (Calls a bellboy over who goes to the trunk to remove luggage, looks at the name on the baggage tags, brings in the luggage and waits near the reception desk.)

## Vocabulary

1. **luggage** [lʌgɪdʒ] n.行李— bags and suitcases and their contents taken on a journey

   *I have 3 pieces of luggage and my friend has 2.*

2. **trunk** [trʌŋk] n.大皮箱— the large box usually at the back end of a car, used for carrying things (British--"boot")

   *We have 4 pieces of luggage in the trunk.*

3. **baggage** [`bægɪdʒ] n.行李— same as "luggage", above

*I have 5 pieces of baggage in the trunk of the taxi.*

# Dialogs

## 2. Introducing the Room and Hotel Services

*After checking in, the guests approach the bellboy.*

A: Good afternoon, Mr. and Mrs. Corning. This is all your luggage, correct?

B: (Checks.) Let me see... yes, that's all of it.

A: Follow me, please. (Walks to the elevator.) After you, ma'am, sir. (Enters elevator.) My name is Zhang Wei. If you have any questions or need some help, feel free to ask me. (Elevator stops.) After you, ma'am, sir. (Exits.)

This way, please.... Here is your room. (Knocks, then opens the door and turns on the light.) After you ma'am, sir. Where shall I put your bags?

C: The little one in the bathroom.

A: Yes, ma'am.

B: The rest just leave on the bed.

A: Yes, sir. May I introduce your room and the hotel facilities?

B: Certainly.

A: The Chinese Hotel is a 4 star property and a favorite of both business and pleasure travelers. On the first floor we have a fine Chinese restaurant and a 24 hour coffee shop serving a wide range of foods, as well as a formal pub bar and an open lounge bar with snacks. On the top floor we have a deluxe Western restaurant serving American and Mediterranean favorites. In the basement we have a swimming pool, sauna, jacuzzi, and a business center. Next to the coffee shop you'll find a gift and souvenir shop and a news kiosk which also offers mail services. On the dresser here you'll find an information brochure including a complete list of services and phone numbers.

The bathroom has an electric razor outlet and phone. On the wall, here, is the thermostat for controlling your room's air conditioning. Here is your closet and minibar refrigerator. Your television has remote control. A tea service is over here by the window. And this bedside console lets you control the radio-cassette player and lights. On the telephone you can find some important numbers. Here is your key, sir.

B: Thank you. How can I contact you?

A: If you need anything, sir, please dial 19 for Housekeeping. Our bar offers a wide range of beers, more than 50 different kinds.

## Vocabulary

1. **introduce** [ɪntrədjus] v.介紹— make known by name; explain something

   *She introduced me to her friends.*

2. **approach** [ əˈprotʃ ] v.接近；靠近— to walk up to; to move near to

   *When I came out of the office, 2 salesmen approached me.*

3. **facilities** [fəˈsɪlətɪs] n.設備— services, aids and/or equipment offered at a place

   *Our hotel offers very good sports facilities.*

4. **property** [ˈprɑpətɪ] n.財產— things owned; buildings and facilities, esp. of a hotel

   *This hotel property is very large, with over 1,000 rooms.*

5. **pleasure** [ˈplɛʒə] n.愉快；高興— feeling of being happy or satisfied

   *It gives us much pleasure to make our guests happy.*

6. **a wide range of** 多種類的— many different kinds; a large selection

   *Our bar offers a wide range of beers, more than 50 different kinds.*

7. **pub** [ pʌb ] n.酒吧— a bar or public house; a place for drinking

   *Tonight, I'm going with a few friends to the pub for a drink.*

8. **lounge** [laʊndʒ] n.休息室— a room or hall with comfortable chairs or sofas; a room to rest

*Since we have to wait, let's go and sit in the lounge.*

9. **Mediterranean** [ˌmɛdətəˈrenɪən] adj.地中海的— having to do with the area of Southern Europe and Northern Africa surrounding the Mediterranean Sea

*There is a wide range of Mediterranean foods to choose from.*

10. **sauna** [ˈsaʊnə] n.蒸汽浴— a steam bath; a very hot room

*We have a sauna near the swimming pool.*

11. **jacuzzi** [dʒəˈkuzɪ] n.漩渦式水流浴缸— a pool of hot, usually turning water, often with bubbles

*After you feel hot in the jacuzzi, you can go into the swimming pool.*

12. **souvenir** [ˈsuvənɪr] n.紀念品— something taken, bought or received as a gift and kept as a reminder of a person or place

*Many people buy postcards to use as souvenirs of their travels.*

13. **kiosk** [kɪˈask] n.公共電話亭— a small building or cabin used as a public telephone or to sell things such as

newspapers

*If you want to buy today's newspaper, you can get one at that news kiosk.*

14. **brochure** [broˈʃʊr] n.小冊子— a printed paper or pamphlet used to give information

*This brochure describes all of our restaurants.*

15. **electric razor outlet** [ìlɛktrɪk][ˈrezɚ][ˈaʊtˌlɛt] n.電鬍刀插座 —special electrical socket used for shaving

*You can find the electric razor outlet in the bathroom, next to the light switch.*

16. **thermostat** [ˈθɝməˌstæt] n.自動調溫器— device used to regulate or control temperature

*Your room thermostat is on the wall next to the light switch.*

17. **minibar** [ˈmɪnɪˌbɑr] n.小冰箱— small refrigerator used to hold drinks

*Every room minibar has 4 cans of soft drinks and 3 cans of beer.*

18. **remote control** [rɪˈmot][kənˈtrol] n.遙控— electronic device used for changing television channels and adjusting the volume

*I'm sorry, sir, our televisions do not have remote control.*

19. **console** [ kənˈsol ] n.操縱台— an instrument panel or unit containing the controls for operating electronic systems
*With this console here you can control the lights, television, and radio.*

# Dialogs

## 3. The Bell Counter

A: (Answering the phone.)  Good afternoon, Bell Counter, may I help you?

B: Hello, this is room 1234.  Why hasn't my luggage arrived yet ?

A: I'm sorry, sir.  May I have your name, please?

B: Arnold, A.R.N.O.L.D.

A: Your room number is 1234?

B: Yes.

A: How many pieces of luggage do you have, sir?

B: 3 suitcases.

A: I will check right away, sir, and call you back.

B: Thank you.

A: (A few moments later.) Hello, Mr. Arnold? This is the Bell Counter. Your luggage is on the way. We apologize for the delay.

#### ························ Left Luggage - No Valuables ························

C: Hi! I'd like to leave my bag here.

A: Yes, sir. We can keep your bag in the storage room. Is there anything breakable or valuable in your bag?

C: No.

A: Thank you, sir. Here is your tag, number 27.

C: What time does this room close?

A: We are on duty 24 hours, sir.

C: Fine. Thank you very much.

A: You're welcome, sir. Have a nice day.

## Left Luggage - With Valuables

C: Hi! I'd like to leave my bag here.

A: Yes, sir. We can keep your bag in the storage room. Is there anything breakable or valuable in your bag?

C: Let me think.... Yes, there is.

A: Sir, we suggest you keep valuables with you or leave them in a hotel safe box.

C: Where are the safe boxes?

A: At the cashier's desk, sir.

C: Thank you. (After removing a few items.) I can leave these here, now?

A: Of course, sir. Here is your tag, number 14.

C: What time does this room close?

A: We are on duty 24 hours, sir.

C: Fine. Thank you very much.

A: You're welcome, sir. Have a nice day.

## Collecting Luggage

D: Hello. I left a bag with you this morning.

A: Yes, ma'am. May I have your tag please?

D: Here you are.

A: Thank you. Just a moment, ma'am.... Here you are.

D: Thank you.

A: You're welcome, ma'am. Have a nice evening.


#### ····················· **Collecting Luggage - Lost Tag** ·······················

D: Hello. I left a bag with you this morning.

A: Yes, ma'am. May I have your tag please?

D: My tag? Oh, right. Let me see. Oh, my, it looks like I lost it.

A: I'm sorry, ma'am, but we must have a tag.

D: But I lost it.

A: I'll ask the assistant manager to come. Please wait a moment.


#### ····················· **Bicycle (or Motorscooter) Rental** ·······················

A: Good morning, sir. May I help you?

E: Yes. I'd like to rent a bicycle.

A: Yes, sir. The charge for 1 day is NT$100.

E: All right.

A: May I have your name and room number, please?

E: Yes. Karl Oxnard, room 4567.

A: Please read and sign this form, sir.... Thank you. Follow me, please. Here is your bicycle, sir. Please return the key when you come back.

E: Thank you.

A: You're welcome.

······································ **A Rainy Day** ································

F: Excuse me? Do you have any umbrellas?

A: Yes, sir. May I have your name and room number, please?

F: Tom Collins, room 4545.

A: Please sign in this book.

F: Here?

A: Yes, sir.  Let me get your umbrella.

F: Is there a charge for this?

A: No, sir. Our hotel offers umbrellas as a complimentary service. Would you like red or black?

F: Black, please.

A: Here you are, sir. Please return it here when you are finished.

F: I will. Thank you.

A: You're welcome. Have a nice day.

**Vocabulary**

1. **apologize** [əpaləˌdʒaɪz ] v.道歉；認錯— to express regret to

somebody for doing something

*I must apologize to you for the things I said last night.*

2. **delay** [dɪ'le] n.延遲— the period of time when something is slowed or made late

*The reason I am late is because my train was delayed 2 hours.*

3. **storage** ['storɪdʒ] n.保管；倉庫— putting things away in a certain place for a period of time

*I wish to put my luggage in storage for the afternoon.*

4. **rent** [rɛnt] v.租用— allow to be used or occupied in return for money

*We own our car, but we rent our house.*

5. **umbrella** [ʌm'brɛlə] n.傘— a small covered frame used to shelter the person holding it from rain

*I'm glad I brought my umbrella because it's started raining.*

6. **complimentary** [ˌkɑmplə'mɛntərɪ] adj.免費的— given free, out of courtesy or kindness

*This is a complimentary magazine given to all our guests.*

**Exercises** ————————————

▸▸ *I. Complete the Dialogs* ◂◂

### 1. Receiving Guests

*A taxi pulls up in front of the Chinese Hotel. The doorman goes forward to open the car door and help the guests out.*

A: Good afternoon, sir.  Good afternoon, ma'am. _____

_____.

B: Thank you.

A: _____?

B: Yes, we are.

A: _____?

B: In the trunk.

A: Yes, sir. If you go in the door, _____.

_____. (Calls

a bellboy over who goes to the trunk to remove luggage, looks at the name on the baggage tags, brings in the luggage and waits near the reception desk.)

## 2. Introducing the Room and Hotel Services

*After checking in, the guests approach the bellboy.*

A: Good afternoon, Mr. and Mrs. Corning. _____

_____?

B: (Checks.) Let me see... yes, that's all of it.

A: Follow me, please. (Walks to the elevator.) After you, ma'am, sir. (Enters elevator.) My name is Zhang Wei.

_____. (Elevator

stops.) After you, ma'am, sir. (Exits.) This way, please .... Here is your room. (Knocks, then opens the door and turns on the light.) After you, ma'am, sir.

_____?

C: The little one in the bathroom.

A: Yes, ma'am.

B: The rest just leave on the bed.

A: Yes, sir. _____

_____?

B: Certainly.

A: (Students should describe in detail their hotel and guest

rooms.)

_____

_____

_____

_____

_____

_____

_____

_____

_____. On the

telephone you can find some important numbers. Here is

your key, sir.

B: Thank you. How can I contact you?

A: _____, please dial 19 for

　Housekeeping. _____.

## 3. The Bell Counter

A: (Answering the phone.) Good afternoon, Bell Counter,

　_____?

B: Hello, this is room 2468. Why hasn't my luggage arrived

　yet?

A: I'm sorry, sir. _____?

B: Keylor. K.E.Y.L.O.R.

A: Your room number is 2468?

B: Yes.

A: How many _____?

B: 2 suitcases.

A: _____.

B: Thank you.

A: (A few moments later.) Hello, Mr. Keylor? This is the

　Bell Counter. Your luggage is on the way. _____

　_____.

········· **Left Luggage** ·········

C: Hi! I'd like to leave my bag here.

A: Yes, sir. We can _____.

   Is there anything _____?

C: No.

A: Thank you, sir. _____,

   number 27.

C: What time does this room close?

A: _____ 24 hours, sir.

C: Fine. Thank you very much.

A: You're welcome, sir. _____.

········· **Collecting Luggage** ·········

D: Hello. I left a bag with you this morning.

A: Yes, ma'am. _____?

D: Here you are.

A: Thank you. _____.... Here you are.

D: Thank you.

A: You're welcome, ma'am. _____.

·················· **Collecting Luggage - Lost Tag** ··················

D: Hello.  I left a bag with you this morning.

A: Yes, ma'am. _____?

D: My tag? Oh, right.  Let me see. Oh, my, it looks like I
   lost it.

A: I'm sorry, ma'am, _____.

D: But I lost it.

A: I'll ask _____. Please wait a
   moment.

·················· **Bicycle/Motorscooter Rental** ··················

A: Good morning, sir. _____?

E: Yes.  I'd like to rent a motorscooter.

A: Yes, sir. _____NT$300.

E: All right.

A: _____?

E: Yes.  Karl Oxnard, room 4567.

A: _____

   _____.... Thank you. Follow me, please. Here is your

motorscooter, sir. _____

_____.

E: Thank you.

A: You're welcome. _____.

················· **A Rainy Day** ·················

F: Excuse me?  Do you have any umbrellas?

A: Yes, sir. _____?

F: Tom Collins, room 4545.

A: _____.

F: Here?

A: Yes, sir.  Let me get your umbrella.

F: Is there a charge for this?

A: No, sir._____.

   Would you like red or black?

F: Black, please.

A: Here you are, sir._____.

F: I will.  Thank you.

A: You're welcome. _____.

————— ▸▸ *II. Classroom Role Plays* ◂◂ —————

1. **Guest:** You arrive at the hotel.

   **Staff:** As the doorman, you help the guest get out of the car and enter the hotel.

2. **Guest:** Your name is Jerry Nittles. You have just checked in and you want to know more about the hotel and room services.

   **Staff:** As the bellboy, you must make the guest feel comfortable and help him understand the hotel and room services.

3. **Guest:** Your name is Robert Santaros. Leave luggage with the bellboy, then come back later to pick it up.

4. **Guest:** Your name is Janet Altos. You first go to rent a motorscooter, but then find that it has started to rain, so you return the motorscooter and check out an umbrella.

## ▸▸ III. Fill in the blanks with the following words: ◂◂

| | | | |
|---|---|---|---|
| returned | guests | beer | thanked |
| storage | enjoy | baggage | pub |
| | airport | luggage | rent |

My name is Zhang and I work at the Bell Counter. This morning one of our _____, Mr. Lindt handed me a piece of _____ and asked if I could put it in the _____ room for him. Then he asked to _____ a motorscooter for the afternoon. After helping him with these things, I returned to my station. Later in the day, he returned with the motorscooter and asked where our _____ is, because he wanted to buy a beer. I showed him, at which time he asked me to get his _____ ready because he would leave for the _____ in a few minutes. On his way out, he _____ me many times for my help. I really _____ helping our guests.

───── ▸▸ *IV. Multiple Choice* ◂◂ ─────

1. When a taxi arrives at the hotel, the doorman should

   _____.

   a. stop the taxi

   b. wave the taxi on

   c. ask the guest his or her name

   d. open the taxi door and greet the guest


2. After a bellboy removes luggage from a taxi trunk, he

   should _____.

   a. check the nametags and wait near the reception desk

   b. take the baggage to the storage room

   c. take the luggage to the guest's room

   d. leave the baggage near the entrance


3. When arriving with the guests at their room, the bellboy

   should _____.

   a. open the door and introduce the room and hotel
      facilities

   b. ask the guests if this is their room

c. knock first, open the door, then let the guests in

d. ask the guests to open the door so he can bring in the luggage

4. If you make a mistake and delay a guest, you should
   _____.

   a. tell him/her not to worry about it

   b. apologize

   c. get angry with the guest

   d. smile, but don't say anything

5. If a guest wishes to use an umbrella, you should _____
   _____.

   a. ask to see his/her passport

   b. first go out to see if it is raining

   c. ask for the guest's name and room number

   d. take the guest's key as a deposit

## ►► *V. Your Hotel* ◄◄

1. What guest services does your hotel offer? What are their open hours?

**Example:** swimming pool 9 a.m. to 10 p.m.

1._____    _____

2._____    _____

3._____    _____

4._____    _____

5._____    _____

6._____    _____

7._____    _____

8._____    _____

2. What restaurants are available at your hotel? What kinds of food do they offer? What are their hours of opening?

**Example:** Alberto's  Western, Italian 11a.m. to 3p.m. and
5:30 to 10 p.m.

1._____ _____ _____

2._____ _____ _____

3._____ . _____ _____

4._____ _____ _____

5._____ _____ _____


3. What do the rooms in your hotel offer?

**Example:** air conditioning

1._____ 2._____ 3._____

4._____ 5._____ 6._____

7._____ 8._____ 9._____

# Unit 3

# Checking In

### Dialogs

### 1. Guest with a Reservation

**B: The guest, Ted Baker, is checking into the hotel.**
**He has reserved a standard room for 3 nights.**

A: Good afternoon, sir. May I help you?

B: Yes. I have a reservation for this evening.

A: May I have your name, sir?

B: Ted Baker.

A: Could you spell your surname, please?

B: Sure. B.A.K.E.R.

A: Yes, Mr. Baker. One standard room. You will be staying 3 nights?

B: That's right.

A: Would you fill out this registration card, please?

B: Yes.

A: Thank you. May I see your passport?

B: My passport? Sure, here you are.

A: Thank you. How will you be settling your account, Mr. Baker?

B: Credit card.

A: May I see your card, please?

B: Yes. Here you are.

A: Thank you. (Gives back the card.) Your room number is 567. The bellboy will show you to your room.

B: Thank you.

A: You're welcome.  Enjoy your stay.

## Vocabulary

1. **check in** [tʃɛk][ɪn] v.登記；記錄— to register or report one's presence at a hotel

   *In order to check in, you must fill in this form.*

2. **registration** [ˌrɛdʒɪˈstreʃən] n.註冊— a record or list of names, often kept in an official book

   *To get a room, you must first go through hotel registration.*

3. **settle (an) account** [sɛtl̩][əˈkaʊnt] v.算帳— to pay for goods or services; to make payment

   *Before leaving the hotel, please settle your account.*

4. **credit card** [ˈkrɛdɪt][kɑrd] n.信用卡— a plastic card used in many businesses instead of money

   *The two most common credit cards worldwide are VISA and MasterCard.*

# Dialogs

## 2. Walk-in Guest

> *B: The guest, Laura Turner, would like a standard room for 2 nights, but has no reservation.*

A: Good afternoon, ma'am. May I help you?

B: Yes. I'd like a single room, please.

A: Very well. Do you have a reservation, ma'am?

B: No.

A: We have standard rooms, deluxe rooms and suites available, ma'am.

B: What's the difference between standard and deluxe rooms?

A: Deluxe rooms are more comfortable with nicer furniture and amenities.

B: How much are they?

A: Deluxe rooms are NT$3000 per night and standard rooms are $2500, and there is a 15% service charge.

B: I'll take a deluxe room.

A: Yes, ma'am. Could you fill in this registration form, please?

B: Certainly. (Hands back form.) Here you are.

A: Thank you. May I see your passport?

B: Yes. Here's my passport.

A: Thank you. How many nights are you planning to stay, Ms. Turner?

B: Just 2 nights.

A: Very well. How will you be paying, Ms. Turner?

B: Cash.

A: Could you leave 2 nights' deposit with us?

B: Yes. How much will that be?

A: 2 nights is NT$6900.

B: Oh, I don't have that much cash. Where can I change money?

A: The Money Exchange Counter is right over there, on your right, Ms. Turner.

B: I'll be right back. (Goes to change money and returns.)

Here's the deposit.

A: Thank you, Ms. Turner. Here is your receipt. Your room number is 789. A bellboy will show you to your room. Please enjoy your stay.

B: Thank you.

## Vocabulary

1. **amenities** [ə'minətɪs] n.優雅；禮儀— things that make life easy and/or pleasant

   *This pleasant city is very modern with many amenities.*

2. **service charge** ['sɜvɪs]['tʃɑrdʒ] n.服務費— charges for food, drink and other services in a hotel, restaurant, or other place of business

   *This price includes a 15% service charge.*

3. **deposit** [dɪ'pazɪt] n.存款；保證金— money or valuables left for safekeeping or as partial payment

   *We must ask you to leave NT$900 here as a deposit before making any long distance calls.*

4. **receipt** [rɪ'sit] n.收據— a slip of paper stating that money

has been paid for something

*This is your receipt for the NT$1000 deposit you left.*

## Dialogs

---

### 3. Overbooked - No Rooms

---

**B: The guest would like to book a room.**

**A: Staff: The hotel is full, so helps the guest find a**
   **room in a nearby hotel.**

B: Hello.

A: Good evening, sir. May I help you?

B: Yes. I'd like a room for tonight.

A: Do you have a reservation?

B: No, I don't.

A: I'm terribly sorry, sir. I'm afraid we are fully booked this
   evening.

B: Are you sure? I just got in from Tokyo and I'm very tired.

A: I can check again for you. (Checks computer.) I'm sorry, sir, but we are fully booked. Would you like for me to check a nearby hotel for you?

B: Yes, please.

A: Would you like a 4 star hotel?

B: Yes, if there's one available.

A: (Gets on the phone.) There are rooms available at the Meridith Hotel. That's not far from here.

B: How much are rooms, there?

A: (Asks on the phone.) A standard room is NT$2400 a night.

B: That's fine.

A: Please write your name here. (Looks.) Meredith Hotel? Yes, we're making a reservation for a Mr. Cornwall. That's C.O.R.N.W.A.L.L. He'll be there in a few minutes. (Turns to the guest.) Mr. Cornwall, you have a reservation and they will hold the room for you.

B: Thank you. How do I get there?

A: Go out the entrance, turn right, and it's just down the

street a little way.

B: Thank you very much.

A: You're welcome. Good night.

## Vocabulary

1. **fully booked** [ˈfʊlɪ][bʊkd] adj.客滿的— the situation where all places are reserved or taken

   *I'm sorry, sir, but our restaurant is fully booked this evening, so there are no more empty tables.*

2. **available** [əˈveləbl] adj.可利用的— capable of being used or obtained; able to get

   *This special food is available only in the morning.*

# Dialogs

## 4. Overbooked - Tonight

> **B: The guest, Sally Peters, is checking in with a reservation.**
>
> **A: Clerk: The hotel is overbooked for this one night only.**

A: Good evening. May I help you?

B: Yes. I'd like to check-in.

A: Yes, ma'am. Do you have a reservation?

B: Yes, for Peters, Sally Peters.

A: Could you please spell your last name?

B: Certainly. P.E.T.E.R.S.

A: Ms. Peters, we are very sorry, but we have overbooked our rooms this evening and we cannot accommodate your reservation. However, we can book you into another hotel and we would cover the taxi fare for you.

B: My reservation is for three nights, and I made it a month ago!

A: We really are terribly sorry about this mistake. Our overbooking is just for this evening, Ms. Peters. If you would like to return tomorrow, we will have a room for you, and we would cover the taxi fare both ways.

B: No, no. I will just stay at the other hotel.

A: Yes, Ms. Peters. Just a moment please and I'll book you into another hotel. Would you like one in this area?

B: Yes. A three or four star hotel, please.

A: (Calls another hotel.) Excuse me, Ms. Peters. I have booked you into the Marxus Hotel, which is right next door to us. It is a 3 star hotel and a standard room is NT$2100 per night. Is that satisfactory?

B: Yes.

A: They are expecting you. I will have a bellboy carry your bags.

B: Thank you.

A: Again, we are very sorry for the inconvenience, Ms. Peters.

## Vocabulary

1. **overbook** [ˌovəˈbʊk] v.過量預訂— to make too many reservations

   *Because the plane was overbooked, 3 people could not get on and had to wait for the next plane.*

2. **accommodate** [əˈkɑməˌdet] v.容納— have; provide; accept; honor; to have space for

   *We can only accommodate 6 more guests because the restaurant is almost full.*

3. **cover** [ˈkʌvə] v.掩蓋；遮蓋— to make up for a mistake by paying for

   *Because of our mistake, we will cover the cost of your dinner.*

4. **inconvenience** [ˌɪnkənˈvinjəns] n.不適合；不愉快— trouble or discomfort

   *Their helping us has given them a lot of inconvenience.*

# Dialogs

## 5. Overbooked - Upgrade

**B:** *The guest, Carl Drexel, has reserved a standard room.*

**A:** *Clerk: The hotel is overbooked on standard rooms, so offers to upgrade to a deluxe room at no extra charge.*

B: Hello.

A: Good afternoon, sir. May I help you?

B: Yes, I have a reservation for tonight.

A: May I have your name, please?

B: Drexel, Carl Drexel.

A: Could you please spell your last name, sir?

B: D.R.E.X.E.L.

A: Thank you. I'm very sorry, Mr. Drexel, but unfortunately we overbooked our standard rooms for this evening.

B: Well, what does that mean? I made my reservation some time ago.

A: Yes, Mr. Drexel. If you'd like, we can upgrade you to a deluxe room but charge you our standard room rate. Is that all right?

B: Sure, that's fine. But my reservation is for 3 nights.

A: We can offer you the deluxe room for all 3 nights.

B: Great. Thank you.

## Vocabulary

1. **upgrade** [ʌpˈgred] v.提高品質— raise to a higher level or grade

   *We can upgrade you from a deluxe room to a suite.*

2. **unfortunately** [ʌnˈfɔrtʃənɪtlɪ] adv.不幸地— having bad luck; being unfavorable

   *Unfortunately, he was on the plane that crashed.*

## *Politeness and Courtesy*

In the hotel service industry,

politeness and courtesy are of the utmost importance.

One of the basic rules of all service industries is that

"the customer is always right." In this case,

that translates to "the hotel guest is always right."

That means, if a mistake is made or there is a

misunderstanding, it is always appropriate for the hotel

staff to apologize for the inconvenience.

This helps to ensure guest satisfaction.

When speaking with guests, standard apologies include:

"we are sorry"

"we are very/terribly/extremely sorry"

"please accept our apology"

# Exercises ────────────────

## ►► *I. Complete the Dialogs* ◄◄

### 1. Guest with a Reservation

---
*B: The guest, Ted Baker, is checking into the hotel.*

*He has reserved a standard room for 3 nights.*

---

A: Good afternoon, sir. _____?

B: Yes.  I have a reservation for this evening.

A: _____?

B: Tom Nakker.

A: _____?

B: Sure. N.A.K.K..E.R.

A: Yes, Mr. Nakker. _____?

B: That's right.

A: Would you _____?

B: Yes.

A: Thank you. _____?

B: My passport? Sure, here you are.

A: Thank you. _____?

B: Credit card.

A: _____?

B: Yes. Here you are.

A: Thank you. (Gives back the card.) The bellboy _____
_____.

B: Thank you.

A: _____.

## 2. Walk-in Guest

> **B: The guest, Lisa Gardner, would like a standard room for 2 nights, but has no reservation.**

A: Good afternoon, ma'am. _____?

B: Yes. I'd like a single room, please.

A: Very well. _____?

B: No.

A: We have standard rooms,_____.

B: What's the difference between standard and deluxe rooms?

A: _____.

B: How much are they?

A: _____

_____.

B: I'll take a deluxe room.

A: Yes, ma'am. Could you _____?

B: Certainly. (Hands back form.) Here you are.

A: Thank you. _____?

B: Yes.  Here's my passport.

A: Thank you. _____?

B: Just 2 nights.

A: Very well. _____?

B: Cash.

A: Could you leave_____?

B: Yes.  How much will that be?

A: _____.

B: Oh, I don't have that much cash. Where can I change money?

A: _____.

B: I'll be right back. (Goes to change money and returns.) Here's the deposit.

A: Thank you, Ms. Gardner.  Your room _____

_____.  A bellboy_____.

B: Thank you.

## 3. Overbooked - No Rooms

B: *The guest would like to book a room.*

A: *Staff: The hotel is full, so helps the guest find a room in a nearby hotel.*

B: Hello.

A: Good evening, sir. _____?

B: Yes.  I'd like a room for tonight.

A: _____?

B: No, I don't.

A: _____.

B: Are you sure? I just got in from Tokyo and I'm very tired.

A: I can check again for you. (Checks computer.) _____

_____?

B: Yes, please.

A: Would you like a 4 star hotel?

B: Yes, if there's one available.

A: (Gets on the phone.) _____

_____.

B: How much are rooms, there?

A: (Asks on the phone.) _____.

B: That's fine.

A: Please _____. (Looks.) Meredith Hotel?

   Yes, we're making _____

   _____

   _____.

B: Thank you.  How do I get there?

A: _____

   _____.

B: Thank you very much.

A: _____.

## 4. Overbooked - Tonight

B: The guest, Sally Peters, is checking in with a reservation.

A: Clerk: The hotel is overbooked for this one night only.

A: Good evening. _____?

B: Yes. I'd like to check-in.

A: Yes, ma'am. _____?

B: Yes, for Waters, Susan Waters.

A: _____?

B: Certainly. W.A.T.E.R.S.

A: _____

_____. However, we

can book you into another _____

_____.

B: My reservation is for three nights, and I made it a month

ago!

A: _____. Our overbooking

is just_____

_____ and we would cover the taxi fare both ways.

B: No, no. I will just stay at the other hotel.

A: Yes, Ms. Waters._____

_____. Would you like one in this area?

B: Yes. A three or four star hotel, please.

A: (Calls another hotel.) Excuse me, Ms. Waters. _____

_____. It is a 4

star hotel and _____?

B: Yes.

A: They are expecting you. _____.

B: Thank you.

A: Again, _____.

## 5. Overbooked - Upgrade

> B: *The guest, Chris Burns, has reserved a standard room.*
>
> A: *Clerk: The hotel is overbooked on standard rooms, so offers to upgrade to a deluxe room at no extra charge.*

B: Hello.

A: Good afternoon, sir. _____?

B: Yes, I have a reservation for tonight.

A: _____?

B: Burns, Chris Burns.

A: _____?

B: B.U.R.N.S.

A: Thank you._____

_____.

B: Well, what does that mean? I made my reservation some time ago.

A: Yes, Mr. Burns. If you'd like, _____

_____. Is that all right?

B: Sure, that's fine. But my reservation is for 5 nights.

A: _____.

B: Great. Thank you.

━━━━━ ▸▸ *II. Classroom Role Plays* ◂◂ ━━━━━

1. B: Guest: Your name is Carla Garland and you arechecking into the hotel. You have a reservation for 5 nights.

   A: Staff: Help the guest check in, getting all necessary information.

2. B: Guest: You walk into the hotel with no reservation.

   A: Staff: There are no rooms available, so help the guest find another hotel.

3. B: Guest: You arrive at the hotel with a reservation for 4 nights.

   A: Staff: The hotel is overbooked, tonight only. Apologize and help the guest find another hotel.

4. B: Guest: You arrive at the hotel with no reservation.

   A: Staff: Help the guest check in.

5. B: Guest: You arrive at the hotel with a standard room reservation for 3 nights.

   A: Staff: The standard rooms are sold out. Offer to upgrade the guest to a deluxe room.

## ►► III. Match the Following Sentences ◄◄

_____ 1. Just a moment please and

_____ 2. We are terribly sorry

_____ 3. I'm very sorry, but unfortunately

_____ 4. If you would like to return tomorrow

_____ 5. We can upgrade you to a deluxe room but

_____ 6. We are very sorry, sir, and

A. we overbooked our rooms this evening.

B. I'll book you into another hotel.

C. we apologize for any inconvenience.

D. about this mistake.

E. we will have a room for you.

F. charge you our standard room rate.

## ▸▸ *IV. Multiple Choice* ◂◂

1. A guest who cancels a guaranteed reservation may_____

   _____.

   a. go home early

   b. arrive earlier than expected

   c. have to pay a cancellation charge

   d. leave later than planned


2. A guest without a reservation is _____.

   a. not welcome

   b. usually given a free upgrade

   c. normally booked into a nearby hotel

   d. called a "walk-in" guest


3. If a walk-in guest arrives at our fully booked hotel, we

   _____.

   a. quickly ask him/her to leave

   b. help him/her find a room in a nearby hotel

   c. upgrade him/her to a deluxe room at no extra cost

   d. ask him/her to wait in the lobby

4. If guests with a reservation arrive at your overbooked hotel, you should _____.

   a. help them find a room in another hotel and cover taxi fare

   b. ask them to wait for a room to open

   c. ask them to look for another hotel

   d. pay for them to stay in another hotel

5. We may offer an upgrade to a guest who_____.

   a. gets angry with our service

   b. wants a better room

   c. has a reservation, but that kind of room is sold out

   d. arrives at our hotel when it is overbooked

6. After arriving at the hotel, a guest should_____.

   a. check in

   b. look for the Assistant Manager

   c. go to his/her room

   d. confirm his/her reservation

————— ▸▸ *V. Politeness and Courtesy* ◂◂ —————

---

In the following conversation between a front desk staff member (A) and a guest (B), the staff member makes several mistakes in the area of polite service. Find the mistakes and change them into acceptable, polite, service English.

---

B: Hello.... Uh, excuse me?

A: Yes, what do you want?

B: I'd like to check in.

A: Do you have a reservation?

B: No. Are there rooms available?

A: Sure. Fill in this form.

B: What kinds of rooms do you have?

A: Nice ones are NT$4000. Cheap standard ones are NT$2300.

B: I'll take a standard room.

A: How many days?

B: Two.

A: Passport?

B: Oh, yeah, right here.

A: You want to pay cash or credit card?

B: Cash.

A: I need a NT$4500 deposit.

B: Okay. Here it is.

A: Okay, Mr. Williams. Here's your key, room 2020.

B: Is there a bellboy?

A: Sure. If you go back to the entrance over there you can find one.

# Unit 4

# Various Front Desk Problems

## Dialogs

### 1. Change of Room

B: Guest: The guest, Dale Simmons, because of problems, wants to change his room.

A: Staff: Helps the guest change his room.

B: Hello.

A: Yes, sir. May I help you?

B: Yes, I need a change of room.

A: Is there a problem with the room, sir?

B: There certainly is. There's a strange odor and the people next door are much too loud.

A: May I know your name and room number, sir?

B: Simmons, Dale Simmons, and I'm in room 3456.

A: Just a moment, please, Mr. Simmons. Yes, we can move you to room 6767. Will that be all right?

B: I'd like to see the room before moving into it.

A: Certainly, sir. I'll call the Assistant Manager to show you.

B: Thank you.

## Vocabulary

1. **odor** [ˈodə] n.氣味— a smell

   *This dog has a very strong odor which gives this room a bad smell.*

## Dialogs

| 2. Change of Room Not Possible |
| --- |

B: Hello.

A: Yes, sir. May I help you?

B: Yes, I need a change of room.

A: Is there a problem with the room, sir?

B: There certainly is. There's a strange odor and the people next door are much too loud.

A: May I know your name and room number, sir?

B: Simmons, Dale Simmons, and I'm in room 3456.

A: Just a moment, please, Mr. Simmons. I'm very sorry, sir, but I'm afraid all of our rooms are fully booked this evening.

B: Well, the room I have now is unacceptable.

A: I will send Engineering and Housekeeping to your room right away to check on the odor, and I will ask the Assistant Manager to check on your neighbors. I hope this will be satisfactory.

B: I hope so, too. We'll see.

## Vocabulary

1. **unacceptable** [ˌʌnəkˈsɛptəbḷ] adj.不能接受的— not acceptable; not satisfactory

   *This beer is very bad; it is unacceptable.*

2. **satisfactory** [ˌsætɪsˈfæktərɪ] adj.滿意的— giving pleasure;
good enough for a purpose; acceptable

   *We think your reasons for not coming are satisfactory.*

3. **leak** [lik] n.漏洞— a hole or crack through which a liquid
or gas may wrongly get in or out

   *These water pipes have many bad leaks, so a lot of water
is lost.*

# Dialogs

## 3. Early Check In

> **B: The guest, Lucy Robbins, has a reservation for 3 nights in a standard room, and arrives early at the hotel.**

A: Good morning, ma'am. May I help you?

B: And good morning to you. I have a reservation for today under the name Robbins.

A: Could you spell your surname please, ma'am?

B: R.O.B.B.I.N.S.

A: Yes, Ms. Robbins. We have you booked in a standard room for 3 nights. Is that right?

B: Yes, that's right.

A: Ms. Robbins, I'm afraid we don't have a room available for you at this time. Several guests have just checked out, so we should have a room for you very soon.

B: I'm really very tired. Are you sure there's no room available now?

A: I can check the computer again for you. (Checks computer.) I'm sorry, ma'am. We were fully booked last night and we've just now been able to start cleaning the rooms. I will phone Housekeeping to see when a room can be made available. Just a moment please. (After phoning.)

A: Ms. Robbins? We can have a room ready for you in about 15 minutes.

B: That'll be fine.

A: Would you like to fill out the registration card, now?

B: All right.

A: How will you be paying, Ms. Robbins?

B: Cash.

A: Thank you. We have a lounge right over there. Would you like to have a seat there while you wait?

B: Sure. Thanks.

A: (After a few minutes.) Excuse me, Ms. Robbins. Your room is ready now.

B: Good.

A: Please follow the bellboy. He'll show you to your room.

B: Thank you.

A: Do have a pleasant stay.

# Dialogs

## 4. Late Check Out

> *The guest in room 4321 wishes to check out late.*

A: Good morning. May I help you?

B: Yes. When is check out time?

A: 12:00.

B: Oh, well, my plane doesn't leave until this evening. Can I check out at 5:00?

A: Just a moment please. I will check our bookings for this evening.... Yes, sir, check out at 5:00 is fine.

B: That's great. Thank you very much.

A: You're welcome, sir.

(Later, another guest comes to ask about late check out, but the hotel is fully booked for the evening, so rooms must be prepared.)

A: Good morning. May I help you?

C: Yes. I want to know whether I can check out about 7:00 this evening?

A: Just a moment please, ma'am. I will check our bookings for this evening.... I'm sorry, ma'am, but our hotel is fully booked this evening. We must prepare rooms for incoming guests this afternoon.

C: But I won't be leaving until this evening. What should I do?

A: We would be happy to hold your luggage for you during the day, ma'am. Otherwise, if you want to stay in the room, we'll have to charge you another 1/2 day of rent.

C: All right. I'll leave my luggage with the bellboy.

**Exercises**

## ▶▶ *I. Complete the Dialogs* ◀◀

### 1. Change of Room

> **B: Guest: Your name is Jerry Xavier and, because of problems, you want to change your room.**
>
> **A: Staff: Help the guest change his room.**

B: Hello.

A: Yes, sir. _____?

B: Yes, I need a change of room.

A: _____?

B: There certainly is. There's a strange odor and the people next door are much too loud.

A:_____?

B: Jerry Xavier and I'm in room 5454.

A: _____. Yes, we can

   move you to room _____, _____?

B: I'd like to see the room before moving into it.

A: Certainly, sir. I'll call _____.

B: Thank you.

## 2. Change of Room Not Possible

B: Hello.

A: Yes, sir. _____?

B: Yes, I need a change of room.

A: _____?

B: There certainly is. There's a strange odor and the people

   next door are much too loud.

A: _____?

B: Jerry Xavier and I'm in room 5454.

A: _____. I'm very sorry,sir,

   _____.

B: Well, the room I have now is unacceptable.

A: _____

_____.

I hope this will be satisfactory.

B: So do I.  We'll see.

## 3. Early Check In

> B: Your name is Mary Chan.  You have a reservation for 4 nights in a standard room, and you arrive early at the hotel.

A: Good morning, ma'am. _____?

B: And good morning to you. I have a reservation for today under the name Chan.

A: _____?

B: C.H.A.N.

A: Yes, Ms. Chan. We have you booked _____

_____?

B: Yes, that's right.

A: Ms. Chan, I'm afraid _____

_____. _____

_____.

B: I'm really very tired. Are you sure there's no room available now?

A: I can check_____. I'm sorry, ma'am

_____

_____

_____

(After phoning.)

A: Ms. Chan? _____.

B: That'll be fine.

A: _____registration card, now?

B: All right.

A: _____?

B: Cash.

A: Thank you. We have a lounge right over there. _____

_____?

B: Sure.  Thanks.

A: (After a few minutes.)  Excuse me, Ms.Chan. _____

_____.

B: Good.

A: _____.

B: Thank you.

A: Do have a pleasant stay.

## 4. Late Check Out

> *B: You are a guest in room 4321 and you wish to check out late.*

A: Good morning. _____?

B: Yes. When is check out time?

A: _____.

B: Oh, well, my plane doesn't leave until this evening. Can I check out at 4:00?

A: Just a moment please. _____

_____.

B: That's great. Thank you very much.

A: You're welcome, sir.

**5. Same as above, but the hotel is fully booked for the evening, so rooms must be prepared.**

A: Good morning. _____?

B: Yes. I want to know whether I can check out about 6:00 this evening?

A: Just a moment please, ma'am. _____

_____. I'm sorry, ma'am, but _____

_____

_____

_____.

B: But I won't be leaving until this evening. What should I do?

A: We would be happy _____

_____. _____

_____.

B: All right. I'll leave my luggage with the bellboy.

## ►► II. Classroom Role Plays ◄◄

1. Early Check In

   B: Your name is Martha Douglas. You have a reservation for 5 nights in a deluxe room, and you arrive early at the hotel.

   A: Help the guest check in early, after a room has been prepared.

2. Change of Room

   B: Guest: Your name is Francis Terrence and, because of problems, you want to change your room.

   A: Staff: Help the guest change his room.

3. Change of Room Not Possible

4. Late Check Out

   B: You are a guest in room 5678 and you wish to check out late.

   A: Staff: The hotel is fully booked for the evening, so rooms must be prepared.

## ▸▸ III. Politeness and Courtesy ◂◂

In the following conversation between a front desk staff member (A) and a guest (B), the staff member makes several mistakes in the area of polite service. Find the mistakes and change them into acceptable, polite, service English.

B: Hello.

A: Yeah?

B: I want to change my room.

A: Why?

B: There's a bad leak by the window and the toilet is broken.

A: That is very hard to believe. Our hotel does not usually have such problems.

B: Well it does now.

A: So why didn't you call Housekeeping?

B: I tried. No one answered.

A: They're lazy people. Anyway, why didn't you look for a housekeeper on your floor? There should be one or two around.

B: Are you going to change my room or not?

A: Okay. Give me your key. Room 3030, eh? Let me check the computer.... Sorry, all the standard rooms are taken tonight.

B: Well, then upgrade me.

A: Do you want to pay more?

B: No.

A: Sorry.No free upgrades.

B: The room right now is unacceptable.

A: Okay, tell you what. I'll find someone in Housekeeping or Engineering to take care of your problems.

B: How long will it take?

A: I don't know. Don't worry. We'll take care of it.

## ▸▸ IV. Unscramble the Following Sentences ◂◂

1. room like I change would to my .

_____

2. name number sir room may know I your and , ?

_____

3. ma'am spell you please could surname your , ?

_____

4. booked evening all I'm of afraid our are this fully rooms .

_____

——————— ▸▸ *V. Multiple Choice* ◂◂ ———————

1. When a guest comes to you with a problem, you should first _____.
   a. call Housekeeping
   b. call the Assistant Manager
   c. offer to change his/her room
   d. try to understand and help the guest

2. If there are real problems with a guest's room, you should _____.
   a. offer to change his/her room
   b. send him/her to another hotel
   c. call Engineering and ask the guest to wait

d. give the guest an upgrade

3. If a guest's room has problems but no other room is available, you should _____.

   a. apologize

   b. help the guest find another hotel

   c. apologize and call Engineering and/or Housekeeping

   d. ask the guest what he/she would like to do

4. If a guest arrives early, you can _____.

   a. ask him/her to wait in the lounge

   b. remind the guest that check in is not until after noon

   c. offer him/her a complimentary breakfast while waiting

   d. see whether any rooms are vacant and ready

# Unit 5

# The Cashier

### Dialogs

---

## 1. Foreign Currency Exchange

---

*Mr. Green goes to the front desk to ask about changing money.*

B: Excuse me?

A: Yes, sir. May I help you?

B: I need to change some British pounds into local currency. Where can I do that?

A: If you walk down the hall this way you'll find the foreign exchange counter on your left.

B: Thank you.

A: You're welcome, sir.

(At the exchange counter.)

B: Hello. I'd like to change 100 pounds. What is the rate?

A: The rate today is NT$45.7 per British pound. May I see the money, sir?

B: Sure. Here it is.

A: Thank you, sir. Please fill in this form and sign at the bottom.

B: Sign here?

A: No, sir. Here, under this line.

B: Right. There you go.

A: Thank you, sir.

B: Oh, by the way, would you mind giving me smaller notes? Maybe 50 and 100 dollar notes instead of 1000's?

A: Certainly, sir. Here you are. Please count to make sure it's correct.

B: Let's see, 50, 100.... Right, 940 dollars. Now, what do I do if I have leftover NT dollars when I leave Taiwan?

A: Be sure to keep this receipt. With this receipt you can change money back at a Bank of Taiwan branch or at the airport.

B: Oh, good. Thank you very much.

A: You're welcome, sir. Have a nice day.

## Vocabulary

1. **cashier** [kæˈʃɪr] n.出納員— person who receives money
   *You can pay for this at the cashier's desk.*

2. **currency** [ˈkɝənsɪ] n.通貨；貨幣— money that is in us in a country
   *The standard currency in America is the US dollar.*

3. **exchange** [ɪksˈtʃendʒ] n., v.交換— the changing of one country's money for that of another
   *You can exchange British pounds for Japanese yen at*

*the money exchange.*

4. **local** [ˋlokḷ] adj.地方性的— special to a place; a certain area

   *This local food is not available in any other city.*

5. **rate** [ret] n.費用；價格— the price or value of something, like currency, in relation to the value of something else

   *Today, the rate for Japanese yen in comparison to French francs is very good.*

6. **note** [not] n.票據— a piece of paper worth a certain amount of money, as in currency

   *This is a 10 British pound note.*

7. **leftover** [ˋlɛftʊˏovɚ] n.殘留的部分— an unused part

   *After paying our bills, we have just $105 leftover.*

8. **branch** [bræntʃ] n.分公司；部門— a natural subdivision; a part of; one of many

   *This company has branch offices in many countries.*

9. **border** [ˋbɔrdɚ] n.國界；邊境— edge; the line marking the division of two countries

   *Some countries, like Japan, have only the ocean for a border.*

# Dialogs

## 2. Checking Out

*Mr. Baird walks up to the front desk check-out counter.*

A: Good morning, sir. May I help you?

B: This is where I settle my account, right?

A: Yes, sir. Do you wish to check out this morning?

B: Yes.

A: May I have your room key, please?

B: Sure.  Here you are.

A: (Checks computer.) Mr. Baird?

B: That's right.

A: Did you use your minibar this morning?

B: No.

A: All right, here is your bill. Please check it.

B: Uh... what's this for?

A: That's a long distance call.

B: Oh, right, right. And this one?

A: Dinner in the coffee shop.

B: Okay, that's right. So, all together 3450 NT$dollars?

A: Yes, sir.

B: Can I pay with traveler's checks?

A: Yes, sir, but you'll have to change them at the money exchange counter.

B: Down the hall, here?

A: That's right.

(A few minutes later.)

A: Ah, Mr. Baird.

B: Right.  Here's the 3450 dollars.

A: Thank you, Mr. Baird. Here is your receipt. We hope you enjoyed your stay with us. Have a pleasant trip home.

B: Thank you.

A: Do come again.

## Vocabulary

1. **traveler's check** [ˈtrævləs][tʃɛk] n.旅行支票 — a safe monetary note issued by a bank or tourist agency for the convenience of travelers

   *When I travel, I never carry money, only traveler's checks.*

# Dialogs

### 3. Counterfeit Bill

> **B: The guest, Mr. McDougall, approaches the money exchange counter.**

A: Good morning, sir.  May I help you?

B: Yes.  I'd like to change 200 US dollars.

A: Please fill in this form, sir.

   (Guest fills in form and hands over the money.)

A: I'm sorry, sir, but this bill is counterfeit.

B: What do you mean?

A: Well, it is not a real 100 dollar bill, sir.

B: What should I do?

A: I'm sorry, sir, but we must keep this bill and send it to the Bank of Taiwan.

B: Well, I want my money. I mean, that's 100 dollars!

A: But sir, it is a fake. We cannot change fake money.

B: Then give it back to me.

A: We cannot do that, sir. I'm sorry, but we must by law send it to the Bank of Taiwan. If you would like, you can speak to the Assistant Manager.

B: Okay.

A: Just a moment and I'll get him.

## Vocabulary

1. **counterfeit** [ˈkaʊntəˌfɪt] adj.假冒的— not real; not true; false; fake

   *When I took this money to the bank, they told me it was counterfeit, and so it is no good.*

2. **fake** [fek] adj.冒充的— counterfeit; not true

   *This is not a real IBM computer; it is a cheap fake.*

**Exercises** ────────────────────

## ▸▸ *I. Complete the Dialogs* ◂◂

### 1. Foreign Currency Exchange

> *B: Guest: Mrs. Thomas goes to the front desk to ask*
> *about changing money.*
> *A: Staff: Help the guest change money.*

B: Excuse me?

A: Yes, ma'am. _____?

B: I need to change some German marks into local currency.
Where can I do that?

A: If you walk down the hall this way _____

_____.

B: Thank you.

A: _____.

(At the exchange counter.)

B: Hello. I'd like to change 500 marks. What is the rate?

A: The rate today is NT$15.2 per German mark. _____

_____?

B: Sure. Here it is.

A: Thank you, ma'am. _____

_____.

B: Sign here?

A: No, ma'am. _____.

B: Right. There you go.

A: Thank you, ma'am.

B: Oh, by the way, would you mind giving me smaller notes? Maybe 50 and 10 dollar notes instead of 1000's?

A: Certainly, ma'am. Here you are. _____

_____.

B: Let's see, 50, 100.... Right, 7600 dollars. Now, what do I do if I have leftover dollars when I leave Taiwan?

A: Be sure to _____. With

this _____.

B: Oh, good. Thank you very much.

A: You're welcome, ma'am. _____.

## 2. Checking Out

> B: Guest: Mr. Cairn walks up to the front desk check-
> out counter.
>
> A: Staff: Help Mr. Cairn check out.

A: Good morning, sir. _____?

B: This is where I settle my account, right?

A: Yes, sir. _____?

B: Yes.

A: _____?

B: Sure. Here you are.

A: (Checks computer.) Mr. Cairn?

B: That's right.

A: _____?

B: No.

A: All right, here is your bill. _____.

B: Uh... what's this for?

A: That's a long distance call.

B: Oh, right, right. And this one?

A: Dinner in the coffee shop.

B: Okay, that's right. So, altogether 3250 dollars?

A: Yes, sir.

B: Can I pay with traveler's checks?

A: Yes, sir, but_____.

B: Down the hall, here?

A: That's right.

    (A few minutes later.)

A: Ah, Mr. Cairn.

B: Right. Here's the 3250 dollars.

A: Thank you, Mr. Cairn. _____.

    We hope _____. _____

    _____.

B: Thank you.

A: _____.

---

## 3. Counterfeit Bill

*B: Guest: Wants to change money.*

*A: Staff: You discover that the bill is a counterfeit.*

A: Good afternoon. _____?

B: Yes. I'd like to change 100 US dollars.

A: _____.

(Guest fills in the form and hands over the money.)

A: I'm sorry, sir, _____.

B: What do you mean?

A: _____.

B: What should I do?

A: I'm sorry, sir, _____

_____.

B: Well, I want my money. I mean, that's 100 dollars!

A: But sir, it is a fake. _____.

B: Then give it back to me.

A: We cannot do that, sir. I'm sorry, _____

_____. If you would like,

_____.

B: Okay.

A: Just a moment and I'll get him.

## ▶▶ *II. Classroom Role Plays* ◀◀

1. Checking Out

   B: Guest: Miss Ratcliffe walks up to the front desk check out counter.

   A: Staff: Help Miss Ratcliffe check out.

2. Foreign Currency Exchange

   B: Guest: Mr. Eerdman goes to the front desk to ask about changing money.

   A: Staff: Help the guest change money.

3. Counterfeit Bill

   B: Guest: Wants to change money.

   A: Staff: You discover that the bill is a counterfeit.

## ►► III. Match the Following Sentences ◄◄

____ 1. I want to change some

____ 2. What is the rate

____ 3. The rate today is

____ 4. Please fill in this form

____ 5. The 50 dolllar charge here is

A. 9 francs per dollar

B. and sign at the bottom

C. pounds into local currency

D. for a long distance phone call

E. for US dollars

## ►► IV. Preposition and article drills: fill in the ◄◄ blanks with appropriate prepositions and articles.

1. I would like ____ change some German marks ____ local currency.

2. Please fill ____ this form and sign ____ the bottom.

3. You can change money at _____ exchange counter _____ the lobby.

4. Walk down _____ hall this way and you'll see it _____ your right.

5. This charge is _____ dinner _____ the coffee shop, and that one is _____ phone call.

# Part II : Food and Beverage

# Unit 6

# Seating and Reservations

## Dialogs

### 1. Seating Guests

*A: The head waiter seats the customers after asking for relevant information.*

A: Good morning, sir. Welcome to the Coffee Shop. A table for 1?

B: No, for 2.

A: Would you like smoking or non-smoking?

B: Non-smoking, please.

A: This way please. (At a table.) How is this table, sir?

B: Fine.

A: (After helping them sit.) Here are your menus. Enjoy your meal.

## Vocabulary

1. **relevant** [ˈrɛləvənt] adj.有關聯的— connected; having relationship to an idea, issue, topic, etc.

   *Do you have all the relevant papers ready for this meeting?*

2. **smoking/non-smoking** [ˈsmokɪŋ][nan] adj.—吸煙的／不吸煙的 areas in a building separated for people who smoke or do not smoke

   *Sir, the toilets are a non-smoking area. Please do not*

*smoke, here.*

3. **menu** [ˈmɛnju] n.菜單— a list, usually printed on paper, of what foods a restaurant offers

   *This month our restaurant is offering a completely new menu.*

# Dialogs

## 2. No Seats Available

> *A: The restaurant is presently full.*
> *B: The guest, Miss Culliver, has no reservation.*

A: Good evening, ma'am. Welcome to the Western Restaurant. Do you have a reservation?

B: No, we don't.

A: I'm sorry, ma'am, but the restaurant is presently full. Would you like to wait a few minutes?

B: How long will we have to wait?

A: I think about 10 to 15 minutes.

B: Where can we wait?

A: Right through this door we have the Pleasant Bar. There is also seating beside the stairs in the lobby.

B: Well, I guess we can wait in the bar.

A: May I have your name to reserve the next open table, ma'am?

B: Yes. Culliver, Nancy Culliver.

A: Could you please spell your surname, ma'am?

B: C.U.L.L.I.V.E.R.

A: Thank you, Ms. Culliver. And how many are in your party?

B: Three.

A: Thank you. I'll call you as soon as a table is ready.

# Dialogs

## 3. Reservation

*A: Receives a phone call for a reservation.*

A: Good afternoon. The Chinese Restaurant. May I help you?

B: Hello, I want to make a reservation.

A: Yes, sir. What day would you like your reservation?

B: Tomorrow evening.

A: And for what time, sir?

B: 7:30.

A: Yes, sir. And for how many people?

B: 5 people.

A: May I have your name, sir?

B: Macken, Thomas Macken.

A: Could you please spell your surname, sir?

B: M.A.C.K.E.N.

A: A reservation for 5 people tomorrow evening, that's June 14, at 7:30 for Mr. Macken. Is that correct?

B: Yes, that's right.

A: Thank you, sir. We look forward to seeing you tomorrow evening.

B: Thank you. Goodbye.

## Dialogs

---
### 4. Reservation - Not Available
---

A: Good evening. The Western Restaurant. May I help you?

B: Hello, I want to make a reservation.

A: Yes, sir. What day would you like your reservation?

B: Tomorrow evening.

A: And for what time, sir?

B: 7:00.

A: Just a moment.... I'm sorry, sir. I'm afraid all of our tables are booked at that time. We have tables available either earlier at 6:00 or later at 7:30.

B: Very well, then. I think we'll book a later table, at 7:30.

A: Yes, sir. And for how many people?

B: 6 people.

A: May I have your name, sir?

B: Jefferson.

A: Could you please spell your surname, sir?

B: Sure. J.E.F.F.E.R.S.O.N.

A: A reservation for 6 people tomorrow evening, that's July 6, at 7:30 for Mr. Jefferson. Is that correct?

B: Yes, that's right.

A: Thank you, sir. We look forward to seeing you tomorrow evening.

B: Thank you. Goodbye.

**Exercises** ————————————————

## ▸▸ *I. Complete the Dialogs* ◂◂

### 1. Seating Guests

*A: Seat the guests after asking for relevant information.*

A: Good morning, sir. _____.

_____?

B: No, for 2.

A: _____?

B: Non-smoking, please.

A: _____. (At a table.) _____

_____?

B: Fine.

A: (After helping them sit.) _____. ___

_____.

## 2. No Seats Available

**B: The guest, Miss Robbins, has no reservation.**

A: Good evening, ma'am. _____.

_____?

B: No, we don't.

A: _____.

_____?

B: How long will we have to wait?

A: _____.

B: Where can we wait?

A: _____. ____

_____.

B: Well, I guess we can wait in the bar.

A: _____?

B: Yes. Miss Robbins.

A: _____?

B: R.O.B.B.I.N.S.

A: _____·_____

_____?

B: 5.

A: _____.

## 3. Reservation

A: Good afternoon. _____

_____?

B: Hello, I want to make a reservation.

A: Yes, sir. _____?

B: Thursday evening.

A: _____?

B: 7:00.

A: _____?

B: 4 people.

A: _____?

B: Curtis, Larry Curtis.

A: _____?

B: C.U.R.T.I.S.

A: _____

_____. _____?

B: Yes, that's right.

A: Thank you, sir. _____.

B: Thank you.  Goodbye.

## 4. Reservation - Not Available

A: Good evening. _____

_____?

B: Hello, I want to make a reservation.

A: Yes, sir. _____?

B: Thursday evening.

A: _____?

B: 7:00.

A: _____.

_____.

B: Very well, then.  I think we'll book a later table, at 7:30.

A: _____?

B: 4 people.

A: _____?

B: Richardson.

A: _____?

B: Sure.  R.I.C.H.A.R.D.S.O.N.

A: _____

_____.  _____?

B: Yes, that's right.

A: Thank you, sir. _____.

B: Thank you.  Goodbye.

---

## ▸▸ *II. Classroom Role Plays* ◂◂

1. Seating Customers

   A: Seat the customers after asking for relevant information.

   B, C: Mr. and Mrs. McAlister want a non-smoking table.

2. No Seats Available

   A: The restaurant is presently full.

   B: The guests, Mr. Stanwick and 3 friends, have no reservation.

3. Reservation

    A: Receive a phone call for a reservation.

    B: Mr. Hull wants to make a reservation for 8:00 tonight for a group of 5.

4. Reservation - Not Available at the Requested Time

    B: Mr. and Mrs. Sharp wish to make a reservation for 7:30 tonight.

## ▸▸ III. Politeness and Courtesy ◂◂

> The following sentences are incomplete or use impolite speech. Rewrite them into polite English.

**Example:** (Answering the Phone.) Hello. Western Restaurant. What do you want?

**Should be:** Good afternoon. Western Restaurant. May I help you?

1. Come here. _____.

2. Smoking? _____?

3. Hi.  2 people? _____?

4. Sorry, the tables are full.

_____.

5. Just wait a few minutes, okay?

_____?

6. What's your name? _____?

7. See you tomorrow. _____.

8. What day do you want a reservation?

_____?

9. Sorry, no tables at that time.

_____.

## ▸▸ IV. Multiple Choice ◂◂

1. If guests arrive when your restaurant is full, you should

_____.

    a. ask them to go to another restaurant

    b. ask them if they would like to wait in another area

    c. tell them to wait in the lounge

    d. tell them to wait in the bar

2. When guests enter the restaurant, you should first _____

_____.

    a. ask them which table they would like

    b. ask them if they want smoking or non-smoking

    c. greet them politely and ask how many are in their party

    d. ask them whether they have a reservation

3. When making a reservation, the important questions to ask are _____.

    a. who (name), when, and where

    b. what day, what time, who, and why

    c. who, what day, what time, and how many people

    d. what time, what day, how many people, and why

4. If a guest calls to make a reservation but no tables are available at the requested time, you should _____.

    a. offer him/her other times that tables are available

    b. ask the guest to go to another restaurant

    c. tell him/her to come earlier or later

    d. let the guest know that the restaurant will be full

5. When a guest calls to make a reservation, before you hang
   up the phone, you should _____.
   a. thank the guest for his/her help
   b. thank the guest for his/her time
   c. ask the guest to please not be late
   d. repeat all the important information for the guest to
      confirm

# Unit 7

# Complaints

## Dialogs

### 1. Misserving

*Ms. King has been seated in the Coffee Shop, has given her order, and is waiting for her food. The waiter approaches.*

A: Your appetizer, ma'am.

B: Thank you. Wait! What is this?

A: A shrimp salad, ma'am.

B: But I ordered a pasta salad.

A: Oh, I'm sorry, ma'am. I'll get that for you right away.

(Waiter takes away shrimp salad and returns a minute later.)

A: Your pasta salad, ma'am.

B: Thank you.

(Later, the waiter brings the main course.)

A: Your steak, ma'am.

B: Waiter?

A: Yes, ma'am?

B: I'm sorry, but this is not what I ordered.

A: Is it not done medium-well, ma'am?

B: That's not the problem. I ordered prime rib with baked beans. This, quite obviously, is T-bone with a baked potato.

A: Oh, I am sorry, ma'am.

(Head Waiter "C" comes by.)

C: Excuse me, is there a problem?

(Waiter "A" explains.)

C: I am very sorry, ma'am. We do apologize for giving you the wrong dish. We'll change it immediately. Can we offer you a complimentary drink while you wait?

B: Well, how long will the steak take?

C: About 10 to 15 minutes.

B: 10 to 15 minutes? I don't have that much time. It's after 7:30 now and I have a meeting in another hotel at 8:00.

C: Are you staying at our hotel, Ms. ...?

B: King. Yes, in room 4040.

C: Ms. King, we really are sorry to have caused you so much inconvenience. How about if we get you a bowl of soup and some bread now, so you won't be hungry, and then when you come back tonight, we'll have room service bring your steak up to your room?

B: That's too much trouble, and I'm not sure how late I'll get back. Maybe I'll just eat this T-bone.

C: I assure you, Ms. King, it will be no trouble for us. After all, it was our mistake.

B: No, no. I'll just eat now.

C: In that case, Ms. King, the entire meal is complimentary.

B: Why, thank you.

A: We really are sorry for this mistake and we assure you it won't happen again. Please enjoy your meal and we hope you have a pleasant stay at our hotel.

B: Thank you.  I will.

---

**Vocabulary**

1. **appetizer** [ˈæpəˌtaɪzɚ] n.開胃菜——a small portion of a tasty food or drink to help the appetite at the beginning of a meal

   *Before the steak comes, I would like to order some cheese as an appetizer.*

2. **shrimp** [ʃrɪmp] n.小蝦—— a small shellfish used for food

   *Look!  There are quite a few shrimps in this salad.*

3. **pasta** [ˈpastə] n.麵糰—— noodles, especially Italian noodles

   *Many people like tomato sauce on pasta.*

4. **steak** [stek] n.牛排—— a thick slice of meat, esp. beef

   *Americans eat much more steak than Asians.*

5. **prime rib** [praɪm][rɪb] n.高級排骨—— a high quality cut of

steak containing rib bone

*Primerib is an expensive cut of steak.*

6. **T-bone** [ˋtiˏbon] n.丁骨牛排— a steak from the short loin with a T-shaped bone

*The largest steak in our restaurant is the T-bone; it is 12 ounces.*

7. **medium-well** [ˋmidɪəm][wɛl] adj.八分熟— to cook meat so none or only a little trace of pink is left in the middle

*I would like my steak done medium-well, please.*

8. **bake** [bek] v.烤— to cook by dry heat

*Some people bake apples and eat them for dessert.*

9. **bean** [bin] n.豆子—seed found in long pods, as in soybeans, kidney beans, etc.

*Beans are a very good food, eaten in most countries around the world.*

10. **potato** [pəˋteto] n.馬鈴薯— a plant with rounded tubers eaten as a vegetable

*Potatoes are a major food source in Northern China and most Western countries.*

11.**immediately** [ɪˋmidɪɪtlɪ] adv.立刻地— not distant; very soon; right now; at once

*I want you to go there immediately, so don't waste any time.*

12. **assure** [əʃʊr] v.確保；保障— say positively and with confidence; to say definitely

*I assure you there's no danger; it's perfectly safe.*

## Dialogs

| 2. Various Complaints |
| --- |

B: Waiter! This is not what I ordered.

A: I'm very sorry, sir. I will bring your order right away.

B: And look at this knife. It's dirty.

A: I'm sorry, sir. I'll get you a clean one .

............................ ✳      ✳      ✳      ✳ ............................

B: Waitress! Look at this! This steak is cold and these vegetables are obviously not fresh.

A: I'm terribly sorry, sir. Let me take this and get you a new one.

······························ * * * * ·····························

B: Waiter! We've been waiting 20 minutes for our food. What's the problem?

A: I'm sorry, sir. I will check on your order right away. (Bringing the food.) Here you are, sir. I'm sorry for the delay.

······························ * * * * ·····························

B: Waitress! I need a spoon to eat my soup.

A: I'm sorry, ma'am. I'll bring you one right away.

B: And don't you have any butter to put on the bread?

A: Oh, that was my mistake. Let me get you some butter.

······························ * * * * ·····························

B: Waiter, there's a mistake on my bill.

A: Where, sir?

B: Here. The coffee I had is included in the dinner special. I should not be billed separately for it.

A: You are right, sir. I'm sorry for the mistake. I'll be back in a minute.

## Vocabulary

1. **spoon** [spun] n.湯匙— kitchen utensil used for stirring, serving, and taking up food

   *Please give me that teaspoon on the table.*

2. **butter** [ˈbʌtɚ] n.奶油— fatty white or yellow food made from milk cream by churning

   *Most Westerners like to eat bread with butter.*

3. **dinner special** [ˈdɪnɚ][ˈspɛʃəl] n.特餐— a special kind of food or a special price offered in a restaurant at dinner time

   *Tonight's dinner special is fresh fish and buttered potatoes for only 350 NT dollars.*

4. **separately** [ˈsɛpərɪtlɪ] adv.個別地— divided; made into

different parts

*We want all the money to be counted separately by two different people.*

5. **knife** [naɪf] n.刀— a sharp blade with a handle, often used in kitchens and at tables to cut

*This knife is too small to cut this watermelon.*

6. **obviously** [ˈabvɪəslɪ] adv.明顯地— easily seen or understood ; clearly

*Look at the food on this spoon. It obviously has not been cleaned.*

7. **fresh** [frɛʃ] adj.新鮮的— new; newly made, gathered, grown, or arrived

*This fish just came off the boat, so it is very fresh.*

8. **check on** [tʃɛk][ʌn] v.檢查— to look into; to investigate

*I don't know what happened to your fish, sir. Let me go to the kitchen and check on it.*

**Exercises** —————————————

## ▶ *I. Complete the Dialogs* ◀

### 1. Misserving

> *Mr. Bradley has been seated in the Western Restaurant, has given his order, and is waiting for his food. The waiter approaches.*

A: Your appetizer, sir.

B: Thank you. Wait! What is this?

A: A shrimp salad, sir.

B: But I ordered a pasta salad.

A: _____

_____.

(Waiter takes away shrimp salad and returns a minute later.)

A: _____.

B: Thank you.

    (Later, the waiter brings the main course.)

A: Your steak, sir.

B: Waiter?

A: Yes, sir?

B: I'm sorry, but this is not what I ordered.

A: _____?

B: I ordered prime rib medium-rare with baked beans. This,

    quite obviously, is well-done and with a baked potato.

A: _____.

    (Head Waiter "C" comes by.)

C: Excuse me, is there a problem?

    (Waiter "A" explains.)

C: I am very sorry, sir. _____

_____

_____

_____?

B: Well, how long will the steak take?

C: About 10 to 15 minutes.

B: 10 to 15 minutes? I don't have that much time. It's after

7:00 now and I have a meeting in another hotel across town at 8:00.

C: _____...?

B: Bradley. Yes, in room 6060.

C: _____

_____

_____. How about if we get you a bowl of soup and some bread now, so you won't be hungry, and then when you come back tonight,_____

_____?

B: That's too much trouble, and I'm not sure how late I'll get back. Maybe I'll just eat this.

C: I assure you, Mr. Bradley, _____

_____.

B: No, no. I'll just eat now.

C: In that case, Mr. Bradley, _____

_____.

B: Well, thank you.

A: We really are sorry for this mistake and _____

_____. Please enjoy your meal and _____

_____.

B: Thank you.  I will.

## 2. Various Complaints

B: Waiter!  This is not what I ordered.

A: _____._____.

B: And look at this knife.  It's dirty.

A: _____._____.

························· *　　　*　　　*　　　* ·····························

B: Waitress!  Look at this! This steak is cold and these vegetables are obviously not fresh.

A: _____._____

_____.

························· *　　　*　　　*　　　* ·····························

B: Waiter!We've been waiting 20 minutes for our food. What's the problem?

A: I'm sorry, sir. _____

_____. (Bringing the food.) Here you

are, sir. _____.

......................... *     *     *     * ..............................

B: Waitress! I need a spoon to eat my soup.

A: I'm sorry, ma'am. _____.

B: And don't you have any butter to put on the bread?

A: Oh, that was my mistake. _____

_____.

......................... *     *     *     * ..............................

B: Waiter, there's a mistake on my bill.

A: Where, sir?

B: Here.The coffee I had is included in the dinner special.

I should not be billed separately for it.

A: You're right, sir. _____.

I'll be back in a minute.

## ▸▸ *II. Classroom Role Plays* ◂◂

1. Misserving

   B: The guest, Mr. Callino has been seated in the Western Restaurant, has given his order, and is waiting for his food.

   A: The waiter comes to start serving the food.

2. Complaints

   Think up and act out a number of different problems that commonly occur in restaurants, and what the proper response of waiters and waitresses should be.

## ▸ III. Make Sentences with the Words Given ◂

**Example:** I / wait / 25 minutes / food

    = I've been waiting 25 minutes for my food.

1. soup / cold / fish / not fresh

    _____

2. not / I / ordered_____

3. drink / included / lunch special

    _____

4. we / offer / complimentary / drink / wait

    _____

5. enjoy / meal / hope / pleasant / hotel

    _____

## ▸ IV. Your Hotel ◂

1. What is your restaurant's policy for handling complaints?

    _____

2. Does your restaurant have a policy for complimentary drinks and meals? What is it?

   _____

3. Which problems should you solve?

   _____

4. Which problems do you need to ask a head waiter or manager to solve?

   _____

# Unit 8

# Complete Restaurant and Bar Dialogs

### Dialogs

---

**1. The Bar - Chinese and Foreign Liquors**

---

*Mr. Arnold (B) and Ms. Johnson (C) enter the bar.*

A: Good evening, sir, ma'am.

B: Good evening.

C: Hi. Nice bar.

A: Thank you, ma'am. Can I get you anything?

B: What drinks does the bar offer?

A: (Handing over a menu.) This is a complete list, sir.

C: A Chinese friend suggested we try a Chinese wine.

A: Yes, ma'am. China has a long history of wine and liquor production. Did your friend mention which kind?

B: What did Mr. Li say? Mao... mao something.

C: That's right. It was Mao Tai.

A: Yes, Mao Tai is a very famous traditional Chinese hard liquor.

C: Oh, it's a liquor, not a wine?

A: That's right, ma'am. Many Chinese people make a mistake when translating the word "wine". Mao Tai is definitely a strong liquor, not a grape wine.

B: You have a good selection of cocktails, I see.

A: Yes, sir.

B: Oh, and quite a few scotches. Hmm, I'll take a Glenlivet.

A: Yes, sir. And for you, ma'am?

C: I think I'll try the Mao Tai.

A: Yes, ma'am. (Gets drinks and returns.) Here's your Glenlivet, sir. And a shot of Mao Tai for you, ma'am.

B: How do I pay?

A: Cash, credit card, or, if you're staying at the hotel, just show me your key and you can sign for it.

B: In that case, I'll sign for it.

A: Thank you, sir.

## Vocabulary

1. **menu** [ˈmɛnju] n.菜單— a list of the dishes available for a meal

   *Please give me a menu so that I may order lunch.*

2. **wine** [waɪn] n.葡萄酒— fermented grape juice; fermented fruit juice

   *Northern California is an area famous for making wines.*

3. **mention** [ˈmɛnʃən] v.提到— to refer to; to speak of

*Did I mention that I saw him yesterday on the street?*

4. **traditional** [trəˋdɪʃən!] adj.傳統的— an inherited pattern of thought or action

   *Shaking hands when meeting is traditional in Western culture.*

5. **liquor** [ˋlɪkə] n.烈酒— a distilled alcoholic beverage

   *This page of the menu lists our selection of liquors.*

6. **translate** [trænsˋlet] v.翻譯— to turn from one language into another

   *If we translate our menus, our restaurants will do better business.*

7. **definitely** [ˋdɛfənɪtlɪ] adv.明確地— certainly; surely

   *We definitely want to eat before going on a long train ride.*

8. **selection** [səˋlɛkʃən] n.選擇— choice; choosing something; what is chosen

   *This menu has a great many selections.*

9. **cocktail** [ˋkɑktel] n.雞尾酒— an iced drink made of liquor and flavoring ingredients

   *One of the world's most famous cocktails is Long Island Iced Tea.*

10. **scotch** [skatʃ] n.蘇格蘭威士忌—a whiskey made in Scotland from malted barley

*Our restaurant has 10 varieties of scotch.*

## 2. Coffee Shop Dialog

A: Good afternoon. Welcome to the Coffee Shop. A table for 3?

B: Yes, that's right.

A: Would you like smoking or non-smoking?

B: Non-smoking, please.

A: This way please. (At a table.) How is this table, sir?

B: Fine.

A: (After helping them sit.) Here is your menu. Would you like something to drink?

B: Yes, I want a beer.

A: We have domestic and imported beers.

B: I'll try a domestic beer.

A: Would you like bottled or draft?

B: Draft.

A: A large or a small glass?

B: Large, please.

A: And you, ma'am?

C: I'll take a glass of white wine.

A: And you, sir?

D: What kinds of juice do you have?

A: We have orange, tomato, and pineapple juices.

D: Pineapple?  Sure, I'll try that.

A: Thank you.  I'll be right back with your drinks.

   (Serving the drinks.)

A: Here are your drinks.  Are you ready to order?

B: No, not really.

A: I'll come back in a few minutes.

(After a few minutes.)

A: Are you ready now?

B: Yes, I think so. I'll take a hamburger.

A: How would you like your hamburger done?

B: Medium-rare.

A: And you, ma'am?

C: What do you recommend?

A: Right now we're having a special on Indian curries.

C: Oh, I don't really like Indian curry. How about the pizza?

A: Certainly. Pizza does take a little longer to prepare and cook.

C: How long?

A: About 20 to 30 minutes.

C: Well, in that case, I'd like the Japanese noodles.

A: Yes, ma'am. And you, sir?

D: I'll have the Sirloin Steak.

A: How would you like your steak done?

D: Medium-well.

B: Oh, and I want a bowl of wonton soup.

A: Yes, sir. Anything else?

C: No, that's fine.

A: Thank you. I'll be back with your orders.

(Presenting the food when it is ready.)

A: Here you are, ma'am, sir, and yours, sir. Enjoy your meal.

(Later, in the middle of the meal.)

A: How is everything?

B: Fine.

C: Quite good.

A: Would you like another glass of beer or wine or anything else?

C: I'd like a cup of coffee.

A: Yes, ma'am. Just a moment, please.

(When they are finished.)

A: Have you finished?

B,C,D: Yes.

A: May I take your plates?

B,C,D: Yes.

A: Would you like some dessert?

B: No, thank you.

D: Well, I would.  Can I see the menu, again?

A: Certainly.  Here you are.

D: Yes, let's see.  What flavors of ice cream do you have?

A: Chocolate, vanilla, and strawberry.

D: Well, that's not very exciting. Hmm. I see here you  have cheesecake.  Is it fresh?

A: Yes, sir.

D: Well, then, I'll take a piece. You, Margaret?

C: No, no.  I'm full. But I will take some more coffee.

D: Just one piece of cheesecake, then.

A: Yes, sir.

(After dessert is finished.)

A: Any more coffee, ma'am? Or anything else I can get for you?

B: Just the bill. (After seeing it.)  I don't think this is our bill.

A: (After looking at it.)  Oh, I'm sorry, sir. I will bring your cheque right away.... Here you are.

B: Yes, this is the right one.  Hmm.  What's this charge for?

A: That's the 15% service charge.

B: Oh, I see.  Can I charge this to my room?

A: Yes, sir. May I see your room key, please? Thank you. Just sign your name, here.

B: Sign here?

A: Yes, that's right. Thank you, and have a nice day.

## Vocabulary

1. **domestic** [dəˈmɛstɪk] adj.國家的— relating to one particular country; not international

   *Taiwan Beer is the main domestic beer in Taiwan.*

2. **imported** [ɪmˈportd] v., adj.進口— something brought from one country into another

   *Many countries import European beers.*

3. **draft** [dræft] adj.生啤酒— beer ready to be drawn from a receptacle (like a keg)

   *Our restaurant offers two kinds of draft beer.*

4. **juice** [dʒus] n.果汁

5. **orange** [ˈɔrɪndʒ] n., adj.橘子

   **tomato** [təˈmeto] n., adj.番茄

**pineapple** [ˈpaɪnˌæpl̩] n., adj.鳳梨

6. **hamburger** [ˈhæmbɝɡɚ] n.漢堡— a sandwich of ground beef patty in a roll

   *McDonald's is the world's most famous hamburger restaurant.*

7. **medium-rare** [ˈmidɪəm][rɛr] adj.五分熟— meat cooked so the middle is still pink

   *I would like my steak done medium-rare.*

8. **recommend** [ˌrɛkəˈmɛnd] v.推薦；介紹— to suggest; to give one's idea or opinion

   *I recommend you not see that movie, because I thought it was bad.*

9. **Indian curries** [ˈɪndɪən][ˈkɝɪs] n.印度咖哩—spice mixes from India

   *My friend likes to eat Indian curries almost every day.*

10. **pizza** [ˈpitsə] n.披薩— a baked open pie made of rolled bread and usually a mix of cheese, tomatoes and meat.

    *My favorite pizza is spicy chicken.*

11. **prepare** [prɪˈpɛr] v.準備— to make ready

    *We should prepare to leave the hotel at 9 am.*

12. **sirloin** [ˈsɝlɔɪn] n.沙朗— a cut of beef taken from the part

in front of the round

*Our restaurant offers a very large sirloin steak.*

13. **wonton** [wʌntʌn] n.餛飩— a kind of Chinese soup dumpling

*Whenever I eat Chinese food, I always order wonton soup.*

14. **chocolate** [ˈtʃakəlɪt] n.巧克力

**vanilla** [vəˈnɪlə] n.香草

**strawberry** [ˈstrɔbɛrɪ] n.草莓

15. **cheesecake** [ˈtʃizˌkek] n.起司蛋糕— a cake made with cream cheese or cottage cheese

*Cheesecake is a favorite Western dessert.*

## Dialogs

---

## 3. Western Restaurant Dialog

---

**H = head waiter    A = waitress   B, C = customers**

H: Good evening. Welcome to the Western Restaurant. Do you have a reservation?

B: Yes, we do.  Table for 2 for Jones.

H: Yes, Mr. and Mrs. Jones. Would you like smoking or non-smoking?

B: Smoking.

H: This way, please.  Is this table all right?

B: How about that one over there? The one next to the window.

H: Certainly, sir.

(Helps them get seated.)

H: Here are your menus. A waitress will be right with you.

A: Good evening. Would you like something to drink?

B: Can we see your wine list?

A: Certainly, sir. Here you are.

B: Umm... a bottle of Glen Ellen white wine.

C: And two glasses of water.

A: Would you like the wine now or with the meal?

B: With the meal.

   (Brings the water.)

A: Are you ready to order?

B: Yes, we are. My wife would like a small salad and the Korean beef barbecue. I'd like the sirloin steak.

A: How would you like your steak done, sir?

B: Medium, please.

A: What kind of dressings would you like with your salads?

B: Thousand Island for me.

C: I'd like Blue Cheese.

A: I'm afraid we don't have Blue Cheese. We do have Franch.

C: No.... How about French?

A: Yes, we do have French. Would you like anything else?

B: No thanks. That'll be all.

   (Waitress returns later with food.)

A: Here you are, ma'am, a small salad and the Korean beef

barbecue. And here is your medium sirloin steak, sir.

B,C: Thank you.

A: Enjoy your meal.

(Waitress returns a few minutes later.)

A: How is everything?

B: This steak is not done well enough. It's too rare. See, it's still quite red in the middle.

A: I'm very sorry, sir. I'll take it back to the kitchen and tell the chef. Anything else?

C: No, mine is fine.

(Waitress goes and returns with the steak.)

A: Here is your steak, sir. Will this be all right?

(Mr. Jones checks the steak.)

B: Yes, this is better.

(After guests have finished.)

A: Have you finished?

B: Yes.

A: May I take your plates?

B: Yes.

A: Would you like some dessert?

C: No, thank you.

B: No, but we would like some coffee.

A: Yes, sir. What kind of coffee?

B: What kinds do you have?

A: We have regular, decaffeinated, cappuccino, and espresso.

B: I'd like a cappuccino.

C: Decaffeinated for me, please.

   (Returns with the coffee.)

A: Here you are.

   (Later.)

A: Would you like more coffee?

B: No, thank you. Just the bill, please.

A: Yes, sir. Here you are.

B: Where do I pay?

A: You can pay me, sir.

B: Here you are.

A: Just a moment, sir. I'll bring back your change.

   (Returns with change and receipt.)

A: Here you are, sir. Have a nice evening.

B,C: Thank you.

## Vocabulary

1. **certainly** [ˈsɝtənlɪ] adv.當然地— surely; definitely

   *We certainly do not have time to see a movie now.*

2. **Korean** [koˈriən] adj.韓國的— from or having to do with the country Korea

   *Do you like Korean spicy noodles?*

3. **barbecue** [ˈbɑrbɪkju] n.烤肉— food cooked over an open fire and/or on a revolving spit

   *Every summer we go to the beach with friends and have a barbecue.*

4. **dressing** [ˈdrɛsɪŋ] n.醬— a sauce for adding to a dish

   **Blue Cheese** [blu] [tʃɪz] n.藍紋乳酪

   **French** [frɛntʃ] n.法國人；法語

   **Ranch** [ræntʃ] n.大農場

5. **coffee** [ˈkɔfɪ] n.咖啡

   — **regular** [ˈrɛgjələ] adj.綜合的（咖啡）

   — **decaffeinated** [dɪˈkæfɪˌnetɪd] adj.低因的（咖啡）

   — **cappuccino** [kɑpəˈtʃino] n.卡布其諾咖啡

   — **espresso** [ɛsˈprɛso] n.濃縮咖啡

# Dialogs

## 4. Chinese Restaurant Dialog

*Mr. and Mrs. Gaines enter the Chinese Restaurant.*

A: Good evening and welcome. A table for 2?

B: Yes. We had a reservation for 7:30 but decided to come a little early.

A: No problem.This way, please.Do you prefer smoking or non-smoking?

C: Non-smoking.

A: Yes, ma'am. How about this table by the window?

C: This looks very nice.

A: (After helping them get seated.) Here is your menu. Would you care to start with some wine or a beer?

B: May I see your drinks list?

A: Certainly, sir.

C: I'll just have tea.

A: Yes, ma'am. (Returns a moment later.) Here is the drinks menu, sir.

B: Hmm. Is this one here a local beer?

A: Yes, sir, it is a domestic.

B: I'll try that, then.

A: Thank you. I'll be right back with your drinks.

(Serving the drinks.)

A: Are you ready to order?

B: There's so much on your menu, it's hard to decide.

C: Can you help us?

A: I'd be happy to. First, let me explain that there are 8 major Chinese regional cuisines. Our restaurant specializes in Cantonese style, but also offers some Sichuan and Beijing dishes.

C: What are the main differences in these styles?

A: Sichuan is famous for its spicy hot dishes, Beijing is well known for its heavy sauces and Peking Duck, while Cantonese food emphasizes light cooking with fresh vegetables.

C: Mm. Can we try one of each style?

B: Sure. Waitress, what would you suggest?

A: For Sichuan style, you might try mapo tofu. It's a tofu dish with a pork chili sauce. For Northern China style like Beijing, you can try jiaozi, which is a meat-filled dumpling. Most of the menu items are Cantonese, so that should be easier for you to choose.

C: How about a vegetable dish?

A: Over here you can see Luo Han, which is a mixture of vegetables.

B: All right.

A: And some rice or noodles?

B: This one here, fried rice with mixed seafood.

A: Yes, sir. Will that be all?

B: All for now.

A: Thank you. (Takes menus.)

# Vocabulary

1. **prefer** [prɪfɚ] v.寧願— to like better; choose above another

   *I like chocolate, but I prefer strawberry.*

2. **explain** [ɪkˈsplen] v.解釋；說明— to make clear; to give the reason for or cause of

   *Could you please explain how to get from here to the zoo?*

3. **major** [ˈmedʒɚ] adj.主要的；重要的— greater in number or importance

   *Salt is one of the major spices in the world.*

4. **regional** [ˈridʒənl] adj.地方的— relating to a certain area or locality

   *Peking Duck is a regional dish of Beijing.*

5. **cuisine** [kwɪˈzin] n.料理— manner of cooking; way of preparing food

   *French cuisine is known throughout the world.*

6. **specialize** [ˈspɛʃəlˌaɪz] v.特殊化；限定— to concentrate in a certain activity

   *At university, I want to specialize in Japanese history.*

7. **spicy** [ˈspaɪsɪ] adj.辣味的— having certain strong flavors

and/or aromas

8. **sauce** [sɔs] n.調味汁— a dressing for salads, meats or puddings

   *Sauces are very important in French cuisine.*

9. **Peking Duck** [ˈpɛkɪŋ][dʌk] n.北京烤鴨

10. **emphasize** [ˈɛmfə͵saɪz] v.強調— giving stress or prominence

    *In our restaurant, we emphasize fast, courteous service.*

11. **suggest** [səˈdʒɛst] v.建議— to recommend; to give one's idea or opinion

    *I suggest you not eat at that restaurant, because I thought it was bad.*

12. **pork** [pork] n.豬肉— the meat of a pig

    *On your pizza, would you prefer chicken, beef or pork?*

13. **chili** [ˈtʃɪlɪ] n.紅番椒—a strong tasting pepper used in hot, spicy dishes

    *Small chilies are usually hotter than the large red chilies.*

14. **dumpling** [ˈdʌmplɪŋ] n.餃子— (usually) a thin sheet of dough wrapping meat and/or vegetables which is cooked

by boiling or steaming

*Pork dumplings are eaten all over China.*

15. **mixture** [ˈmɪkstʃɚ] n.混合物— several things which are combined into one

    *Cocktails are often a mixture of liquor, soda and/or fruit juice.*

16. **rice** [raɪs] n.米飯

17. **fried rice** [fraɪd][raɪs] n.油飯

18. **noodles** [ˈnudl̩s] n.麵

19. **seafood** [ˈsiˌfud] n.海鮮— food from the sea

    *Fish, crab and lobsters are all favorite seafoods.*

# *Polite English —*
# *"would you like" and*
# *"would you care for"*

Although commonly used in daily speech, the English form "do you want" is not considered polite and appropriate in the service industry.
When asking a guest's preferences, the service person should use one of the two polite forms "would you like" or "would you care for".

## *Examples*

1. Would you like another cup of coffee, sir?

2. Would you care for dessert, ma'am?

# *Relative Pronouns:*
# *who, which, that, where*

Relative pronouns are used in English to describe a preceding noun.
"Who" is used when describing a person.

### *Examples*

This is the boy who won first prize in the writing contest.

In the example, all the words following "who" are used to describe or identify the preceding noun "boy". This helps the reader to know which boy is being discussed. "Which" and "that" are interchangeable and are used to describe things, not people.

### *Examples*

This is the chair which I broke.

This is the chair that I broke.

Again, the words following "which" and "that" are simply identifying which chair was broken. "Where" is used when describing places.

### *Examples*

This is the table where I put your bags.

I am going to the room where

the police are waiting.

**Exercises** ————————————

## ▶▶ *I. Complete the Dialogs* ◀◀

### 1. The Bar - Chinese and Foreign Liquors

> *Mr. Keynes (B) and Ms. Allison (C) enter the bar.*

A: Good evening, sir, ma'am.

B: Good evening.

C: Hi.  Nice bar.

A: Thank you, ma'am. _____?

B: What drinks does the bar offer?

A: (Handing over a menu.)_____.

C: A Chinese friend suggested we try a local wine.

A: Yes, ma'am.  China has _____

_____. Did your friend _____

_____?

B: What did Mr. Li say?  Mao... mao something.

C: That's right.  It was Mao Tai.

A: Yes, Mao Tai is a _____.

C: Oh, it's a liquor, not a wine?

A: That's right, ma'am. Many Chinese people make a mistake when translating the word "wine". Mao Tai is

_____.

B: You have a good selection of cocktails, I see.

A: Yes, sir.

B: Oh, and quite a few scotches.  Hmm, I'll take a Johnny Walker.

A: Yes, sir.  And for you, ma'am?

C: I think I'll have Mao Tai.

A: Yes, ma'am. _____, sir.  And a glass of _____.

B: How do I pay?

A: _____

_____.

B: In that case, I'll sign for it.

A: Thank you, sir.

## 2. Coffee Shop Dialog

**A = waitress     B, C, D = guests**

A: Good afternoon. _____ ?

B: Yes, that's right.

A: _____ ?

B: Smoking, please.

A: _____. (At a table.) _____ ?

B: Fine.

A: (After helping them sit.) _____. _____

_____ ?

B: Yes, I want a beer.

A: _____ .

B: I'll try a domestic beer.

A: _____ ?

B: Bottled.

A: _____ ?

B: Large, please.

A: And you, ma'am?

C: I'll take a glass of red wine.

A: And you, sir?

D: What kinds of juice do you have?

A: _____.

D: Strawberry? Sure, I'll try that.

A: Thank you. _____.

   (Serving the drinks.)

A: Here are your drinks. _____?

B: No, not really.

A:_____.

   (After a few minutes.)

A: _____?

B: Yes, I think so. I'll take a hamburger.

A: _____?

B: Medium-rare.

A: And you, ma'am?

C: What do you recommend?

A: _____.

C: Oh, I don't really like Indian curry. How about the
   pizza?

A: _____.

C: How long?

A: _____.

C: Yes, that's fine.

A: Yes, ma'am.  And you, sir?

D: I'll have the T-bone steak.

A: _____?

D: Medium-well.

B: Oh, and I want a bowl of chicken soup.

A: Yes, sir.  Anything else?

C: No, that's all.

A: _____.

   (Presenting the food when it is ready.)

A: _____.

   (Later, in the middle of the meal.)

A: _____?

B: Fine.

C: Quite good.

A: _____?

C: I'd like a cup of coffee.

A: Yes, ma'am. _____.

   (When they are finished.)

A: _____?

B,C,D: Yes.

A: _____?

B,C,D: Yes.

A: _____?

B: No, thank you.

D: Well, I would.  Can I see the menu, again?

A: _____.

D: Yes, let's see.  What flavors of ice cream do you have?

A: _____.

D: Well, that's not very exciting. Hmm. I see here you have cheesecake.  Is it fresh?

A: Yes, sir.

D: Well, then, I'll take a piece.  You, Margaret?

C: No, no.  I'm full.  But I will take some more coffee.

D: Just one piece of cheesecake, then.

A: Yes, sir.

(After dessert is finished.)

A: Any more coffee ma'am? _____?

B: Just the bill. (After seeing it.) I don't think this is our bill.

A: (After looking at it.) _____. _____

_____.

B: Yes, this is the right one.  Hmm.  What's this charge for?

A: That's the 15% service charge.

B: Oh, I see.  Can I charge this to my room?

A: _____? _____

_____.

B: Sign here?

A: Yes, that's right.  Thank you, and have a nice day.

## 3. Western Restaurant Dialog

**H = head waiter   A = waitress   B, C = customers**

H: Good evening. _____

_____?

B: Yes, we do.  Table for 2 for Peters.

H: Yes, Mr. and Mrs. Peters. _____

_____?

B: Non-smoking, please.

H: _____?

B: How about that one over there?

H: Certainly, sir.

(Helps them get seated.)

H: Here are your menus. _____ .

A: Good evening. _____?

B: Can we see your wine list?

A: Certainly, sir.

B: Umm... a bottle of Beringer red wine.

C: And two glasses of water.

A: Would you like the wine now or with the meal?

B: With the meal.

(Brings the water.)

A: _____?

B: Yes, we are. My wife would like a small salad and the Korean lamb. I'd like the tenderloin steak.

A: _____?

B: Medium-rare, please.

A: _____?

B: No thanks. That'll be all.

(Waitress returns later with food.)

A: _____

_____.

What kind of dressing would you like for your salad? (Waitress presents the different dressings, allowing the customer to choose.)

C: Thank you.

A: _____.

(Waitress returns a few minutes later.)

A: _____?

B: This steak is overdone. It's not medium-rare. See, it's quite grey in the middle.

A: _____

_____. _____?

C: No, mine is fine.

(Waitress goes and returns with a new steak.)

A: Here is your steak, sir. Will this be all right?

(Mr. Jones checks the steak.)

B: Yes, this is better.

(After guests have finished.)

A: _____?

B: Yes.

A: _____?

B: Yes.

A: _____?

C: No, thank you.

B: No, but we would like some coffee.

A: Yes, sir. _____?

B: What kinds do you have?

A: _____.

B: I'd like an espresso.

C: Decaffeinated, please.

  (Returns with the coffee.)

A: Here you are.

  (Later.)

A: _____?

B: No, thank you.  Just the bill, please.

A: Yes, sir.  Here you are.

B: Where do I pay?

A: _____.

B: Here you are.

A: Just a moment, sir. _____.

  (Returns with change and receipt.)

A: Your change, sir.

B,C: Thank you.

## 4. Chinese Restaurant Dialog

---

*Mr. and Mrs. Belcher enter the Chinese Restaurant.*

---

A: Good evening and welcome. _____?

B: Yes. We had a reservation for 7:30 but decided to come a little early.

A: No problem. This way please. _____

_____?

C: Non-smoking.

A: Yes, ma'am. _____?

C: This looks very nice.

A: (After helping them get seated.) Here is your menu. ____

_____?

B: May I see your drinks list?

A: Certainly, sir.

C: I'll just have tea.

A: Yes, ma'am. (Returns a moment later.) _____

_____.

B: Hmm. Is this one here a local beer?

A: Yes, sir, it is.

B: I'll try that, then.

A: Thank you. _____.

   (Serving the drinks.)

A: _____?

B: There's so much on your menu, it's hard to decide.

C: Can you help us?

A: I'd be happy to. First, let me explain _____

   _____.Our restaurant _____

   _____, but also offers _____

   _____.

C: What's the main differences in these styles?

A: Sichuan is _____, Beijing is

   well _____

   _____, while Cantonese food_____

   _____.

C: Mm. Can we try one of each style?

B: Sure. Waitress, what would you suggest?

A: For Sichuan style, _____. It's a tofu

   dish _____. For Northern

China style, like Beijing, you _____

_____. Most of the menu

items are Cantonese, so that should be easier for you to

choose.

C: How about a vegetable dish?

A: Over here you can see Luo Han, _____

_____.

B: All right.

A: _____?

B: This one here, fried rice with mixed seafood.

A: Yes, sir. _____?

B:. All for now.

A: Thank you. (Takes menus.)

## ▸▸ *II. Classroom Role Plays* ◂◂

1. The Bar— Chinese and Foreign Liquors

   The guests, Mr. Kyle (B) and Ms. Leffert (C) enter

   the bar.

   A: Bartender: Serve the guests.

2. Make a complete Coffee Shop dialog.

The guests, Mr. and Mrs. Presley (B, C) enter the Coffee Shop.

3. Do a complete Western Restaurant dialog.

The guests, Mr. and Mrs. Wilcox (B, C) enter the Western Restaurant.

4. Create and act out a complete Chinese Restaurant dialog.

Mr. and Mrs. Corinth (B, C) enter the Chinese Restaurant.

## ▸▸ III. Fill in the blanks with the relative ◂◂ pronouns: who, which, that, where

1. Beijing has many famous places, the most famous of _____ are the Forbidden City and the Great Wall.

2. He's the waiter _____ found the key I lost.

3. This hotel, _____ was built in 1935, is still in very good condition.

4. Do you have a waitress _____ can speak English?

5. This is the restaurant _____ John Wayne ate.

6. Our Presidential Suite is the room _____ has the largest T.V..

7. Isn't he the one _____ stayed in the deluxe suite last week?

8. We walked to the corner _____ the bus stops.

— ▸▸ *IV. Unscramble the Following Sentences* ◂◂ —

1. like you drink would something to ?

_____

2. you order are to ready ?

_____

3. steak like you done how your would ?

_____

4. pizza right having on we're special now a .

_____

5. in styles our of food Sichuan restaurant and Cantonese specializes .

_____

6. to menu much so there's on it's your decide hard , .

_____

────────── ▸▸ *V. Politeness and Courtesy* ◂◂ ──────────

In the following conversation between a waiter and guest, the waiter makes several mistakes in the area of polite service. Find the spoken mistakes and change them into acceptable, polite, service English. Mistakes in service should be noted for class discussion.

**Scene** Mr. Wyatt arrives at the entrance of the restaurant. A waiter approaches.

A: A table for 1?

B: Yes.

A: Sit here, please.

B: Thanks.

A: Here's your menu. What do you want to drink?

B: What do you have?

A: You know, beer, baijiu, wine, juices, coffee.

B: Okay. What kind of beer?

A: Imported and domestic.

B: Imported.

A: We have Becks, Heinecken, Fosters and Guinness.

B: Becks.

A: And what do you want to eat?

B: What would you recommend?

A: Read the menu. It's all there.

B: Thanks a lot. What's this?

A: That's our special soup.

B: Okay, give me some soup, and this one here, chicken with cashews.

A: Some rice?

B: Yes, one bowl.

A: Anything else?

B: No, thanks.

———————— ▸▸ *VI. Your Hotel* ◂◂ ————————

1. What are the restaurants in your hotel?

   _____

   _____

   _____

   _____

2. What hours are they open?

   _____

   _____

   _____

   _____

3. What kinds of food do they serve?

   _____

   _____

   _____

   _____

   _____

   _____

4. What beers and wines does your hotel offer?

_____

_____

_____

_____

_____

_____

# Part III : Housekeeping

# Unit 9

# The Room

### Dialogs

## 1. Making up the Room

*A room attendant with a housekeeping trolley knocks on the Naders' door.*

A: Good morning. Housekeeping.

B: Yes?

A: Good morning, Mrs. Nader. Would you like me to make up your room now or later?

B: Well, I suppose now is okay. We're just about to leave.

A: Yes, ma'am.

B: Oh! Could you be sure to check the shampoo? I think we're out.

C: (Mr. Nader walks up to the door.) And don't forget the tea. We're having guests over tonight.

A: Yes, sir. Would you like for me to arrange for flowers, fruit, or some drinks for your guests?

B: Some flowers would be nice, wouldn't they, Bill?

C: Sure, honey. Yes, some flowers, please.

B: And could you bring us 2 more cups for tea?

A: Yes, ma'am. I can have the flowers brought in this afternoon.

B: That'll be fine.

A: Have a nice day.

# Vocabulary

1. **trolley** [ˈtrɑlɪ] n.貨車— a wheeled carriage used to carry things

   *Every trolley should be refilled each morning before cleaning rooms.*

2. **make up** [mek][ʌp] v.整理；組織— to clean; to put in order

   *Every morning, room attendants must make up all the rooms.*

3. **shampoo** [ʃæmˈpu] n.洗髮精— liquid soap used for cleaning hair

   *Every guest bathroom should have two small bottles of shampoo.*

4. **arrange (for)** [əˈrendʒ] v.籌備；安排— to order; to set up; to plan; to prepare

   *We will hold a party tomorrow and we need to arrange for some music.*

# Dialogs

## 2. Requests

---

*A guest calls the Housekeeping office.*

---

A: Good evening. Housekeeping. May I help you?

B: Yes. We're having some friends over this evening and we'd like some ice and hot water. Oh, and some more tea bags.

A: Yes, sir.

B: And also some more glasses and cups. Maybe 3 or 4 of each.

A: Yes, sir. May I know your room number so I can send someone there right away?

B: Yes. We're in room 7654. Thank you.

A: You're welcome, sir.

......................... \*     \*     \*     \* ..........................

A: Good morning. Housekeeping. May I help you?

B: Yes. Our children were out playing this morning and got quite dirty. We're going to need more soap and towels.

A: Yes, ma'am. Anything else?

B: Oh, yes. More toilet paper. And could you bring up the morning paper?

A: Certainly. May I know your room number so I can send someone?

B: Of course. We're in room 8923.

A: 8923. We'll be there right away.

B: Thank you so much.

A: You're welcome, ma'am.

## Vocabulary

1. **ice** [aɪs] n.冰

   *Use ice if you want a cold drink.*

2. **tea bag** [ti][bæg] n.茶袋— a small bag containing tea leaves or grains

   *This tea bag has been used, so I will need a new one.*

3. **play** [ple] v.玩；遊戲

*Children like to play all day long.*

4. **quite** [kwaɪt] adj.完全的；徹底的— completely; fully; wholly; really

*This steak is quite good, and I am quite happy.*

5. **dirty** [ˋdɝtɪ] adj.髒的— not clean

*After children play outside, they often are quite dirty.*

6. **towel** [ˋtauəl] n.毛巾；紙巾

*Place clean towels in the guest bathrooms every day.*

7. **soap** [sop] n.肥皂

*If you want to get clean, it's best to use soap when you wash.*

8. **toilet paper** [ˋtɔɪlɪt][ˋpepɚ] n.衛生紙— tissue paper; paper used in the toilet

*Every trolley should have clean towels, shampoo, soap, and toilet paper.*

9. **(news) paper** [ˋnjuz][͵pepɚ] n.報紙— a paper printed regularly and containing news and other information of immediate interest

*The New York Times is one of the world's largest newspapers.*

*Our hotel offers a complimentary paper to every guest.*

# Dialogs

## 3. Problems

*A guest calls the Housekeeping office.*

A: Good afternoon. Housekeeping. May I help you?

B: Yes. This is room 1234. My bathroom was not cleaned properly and my minibar is not stocked.

A: I'm sorry, sir. I will send someone to your room right away.

B: Oh, also, I'd like to get an iron to press my clothes.

A: I'm sorry, sir. Because of hotel and city fire regulations, guests are not allowed to use irons in the rooms.

B: But I need to press my clothes.

A: Our laundry has a pressing service, sir.

B: How much is it?

A: If you look in your dresser drawer, you will see a form to fill out which includes prices.

B: Well, I need this done right away.

A: I'll ask a housekeeper to go to your room and pick up your clothes.

B: All right. Thank you.

A: You're welcome, sir.

**A guest meets a housekeeper in the hall.**

B: Excuse me?

A: Yes, sir. May I help you?

B: I seem to have left my key in the room. Could you open the door for me, please?

A: I'm sorry, sir, but for security reasons, I'm not allowed to open rooms for guests. If you go to the front desk, the Assistant Manager can open your room for you.

B: Oh. Well, thanks.

(Returning with the Assistant Manager.)

A: Is this your room, sir?

B: Yes.

A: (Opens the door.) Let's try to find your key.

B: Here it is, on top of the television. Oh, that reminds me. The TV seems to be having a problem.

A: What sort of problem, sir?

B: It won't pick up some stations.

A: (Tries to fix it, but doesn't work.) I'll contact maintenance for you, sir. Anything else?

B: Uh, let's see. Oh! Can I get a hair dryer?

A: Yes. I'll have Housekeeping bring one over.

B: Thanks for all your help.

A: You're welcome, sir. Have a pleasant stay.

## Vocabulary

1. **properly** [ˈprɑpəlɪ] adv.正確地— correctly; in the right way
   *Every room attendant must learn to properly clean a room.*

2. **stock** [stɑk] v.庫存— filled; available; on hand
   *Every guest bathroom should be stocked with clean towels, shampoo, soap and toilet paper.*

3. **iron** [ˈaɪən] n.熨斗
   *Guests are not allowed to use irons in their rooms.*

4. **press** [prɛs] v.壓— to push; to make flat
   *Our hotel laundry offers a service for pressing clothes.*

5. **drawer** [ˈdrɔə] n.抽屜— a place for keeping clothes and other articles, which usually can be pulled out, and often

stacked several high

*If you look in the desk drawer, you will find some letter paper.*

6. **form** [fɔrm] n.表格— a document with blank spaces for writing in answers or making requests

*When leaving clothes for cleaning, please fill in the laundry form.*

7. **security** [sɪˋkjurətɪ] n.安全— safety; what is done for protection

*For security, we ask guests to leave valuables in the hotel safe box.*

8. **reason** [ˋrizn̩] n.理由；原因— a cause; an explanation; the thinking behind something

*For health reasons, I do not smoke.*

9. **allow** [əˋlaʊ] v.允許— to let; to permit; to approve; to say something can be done

*We do not allow smoking in some of our guest rooms.*

10. **(TV) station** [ˋsteʃən] n.台— company which sends out television programs

*We used to have only four TV stations, but now there are over fifty.*

11. **contact** [ˋkantækt] v.接觸— to get in touch; speak to; call

    *I haven't been in contact with this friend for two years,*
    *so I am happy he called me yesterday.*

12. **hair dryer** [hɛr] [ˋdraɪɚ] n.吹風機— machine for blowing
    air to dry the hair

    *All bathrooms in the hotel suites have hair dryers.*

**Exercises** ——————————————

## ▸▸ *I. Complete the Dialogs* ◂◂

### 1. Making up the Room

> *A room attendant with a trolley knocks on the Campbell's door.*

A: Good morning. _____.

B: Yes?

A: Good morning, Mrs. Campbell. _____

_____?

B: Well, I suppose now is okay. We're just about to leave.

A: Yes, ma'am.

B: Oh! Could you be sure to check the shampoo? I think we're out.

C: (Mr. Campbell walks up to the door.) And don't forget the tea. We're having guests over tonight.

A: Yes, sir.  Would you like _____

_____?

B: Some drinks would be nice, wouldn't they, John?

C: Sure, honey. Yes, some drinks, please. Maybe a bottle of wine with some wine glasses.

A: Would you like a local wine or _____

_____?

C: Oh... maybe an imported wine. Maybe a French white wine?  Yes, that should do.

B: And could you bring us 2 more cups for tea?

A: Yes, ma'am.  _____

_____ brought in this afternoon.

B: That'll be fine.

A: _____.

## 2. Requests

A guest calls the Housekeeping office.

A: Good evening. _____?

B: Yes. We're having some friends over this evening and we'd like some ice and hot water. Oh, yes. And some more tea bags.

A: Yes, sir.

B: And also some more glasses and cups. Maybe 3 or 4 of each.

A: Yes, sir. May I know _____

_____?

B: Yes. We're in room 7654. Thank you.

A: _____.

·························· *    *    *    * ··························

A: Good morning. _____?

B: Yes. Our children were out playing this morning and got quite dirty. We're going to need more soap and towels.

A: Yes, ma'am. _____ else?

B: Oh, yes. More toilet paper. And could you bring up the morning paper?

A: Certainly. _____

_____?

B: Of course.  We're in room 9753.

A: _____.

B: Thank you so much.

A: _____.

## 3. Problems

r--------------------------------------------
|  *A guest calls the housekeeping office.*
L--------------------------------------------

A: Good afternoon.  _____?

B: Yes.  This is room 1234. My bathroom was not cleaned properly and my minibar is not stocked.

A: _____.  I will send_____

_____.

B: Oh, also, I'd like to get an iron to press my clothes.

A: I'm sorry, sir. Because of hotel and city fire regulations,

_____.

B: But I need to press my clothes.

A: _____.

B: How much is it?

A: If you look in _____

_____.

B: Well, I need this done right away.

A: I'll ask a housekeeper _____

_____.

B: All right.  Thank you.

A: _____.

················· *     *     *     * ···· ··········

*A guest meets a housekeeper in the hall.*

B: Excuse me?

A: Yes, sir.  _____?

B: I seem to have left my key in the room. Could you open
the door for me, please?

A: I'm sorry, sir.  But for security _____

_____.  If you go to the

front desk, _____.

B: Oh. Well, thanks.

(Returning with the Assistant Manager.)

A: Is this your room, sir?

B: Yes.

A: (Opens the door.) Let's try to find your key.

B: Here it is, on top of the television. Oh, that reminds me.

The TV seems to be having a problem.

A: _____?

B: It won't pick up some stations.

A: (Tries to fix it, but doesn't work.) _____

_____. Anything else?

B: Uh, let's see. Oh! Can I get a hair dryer?

A: Yes. I'll have _____.

B: Thanks for all your help.

A: You're welcome. _____.

————— ▸▸ *II. Classroom Role Plays* ◂◂ —————

1. Requests

    B: You are the guest, Mrs. Brown. Call Housekeeping and make several requests.

    A: As a Housekeeping staff, respond properly to each request.

2. Making up a room

    A: You are a room attendant with a cleaning trolley. Knock on the Edwards' door.

3. Problems

    B: You are the guest, Mr. Cranston. Call the House-keeping office to report several problems.

    A: Respond properly to each problem.

## — ▸▸ *III. Unscramble the Following Sentences* ◂◂ —

1. your may so send can know someone I room I number , ?

   _____

2. away be right we'll there .

   _____

3. more we shampoo need and soap some .

   _____

4. right will I away room send to someone your .

   _____

5. rooms not guests security for I'm open to allowed reasons for .

   _____

6. I'll you maintenance sir for contact , .

   _____

## ▸▸ IV. Multiple Choice ◂◂

1. When entering a guest's room to clean, a housekeeper should _____.

   a. open the door and turn on the light

   b. open the door, check the room, then turn on the light

   c. knock and open the door

   d. knock, say "Housekeeping", wait a moment, then enter

2. If a guest mentions he/she will have guests over, a house-keeper should _____.

   a. ask who the guests are

   b. ask where the guests are staying

   c. offer to have flowers, fruit and/or drinks brought

   d. offer to help the guests find a room

3. When taking information on the phone, it is important to ask _____.

   a. the guest's room number

   b. how long the guest will be staying

   c. the guest's name

d. if the guest would like hot water

4. If a guest asks for something which is not allowed (like an iron), it is good for a housekeeper to _____.
   a. send someone to the guest's room
   b. let the guest have it, anyway
   c. ask the guest to talk with the Assistant Manager
   d. explain why it is not allowed and offer an alternative

5. If a guest asks a housekeeper to open his/her room, the housekeeper should _____.
   a. open the door to let the guest in
   b. call the Assistant Manager while the guest waits in the room
   c. explain why he/she can't and ask the guest to contact the Assistant Manager
   d. ask to see the guest's passport

# Unit 10

# Services

### 1. Convenient Services

---

*A guest calls Housekeeping.*

---

A: Good afternoon.  Housekeeping.

B: Hello.  I just came from the airport and I have a meeting in a few hours.  Do you have any razors?

A: We don't have electric razors, but we do have straight edge razors.

B: That's fine.  And how about hair dryers?

A: Yes, sir.  We do have hair dryers.

B: Good, good.  Let me see.... anything else.  Oh, yes.  What about a shoe shine service?

A: Our hotel offers a complimentary shoe shine service to our guests. We can pick up your shoes when we deliver the razor and hair dryer.

B: That's fine.

A: Anything else, sir?

B: No, that'll be all for now.

A: I'll send someone right away.

B: Thank you.

A: You're welcome, sir. Enjoy your stay.

## Vocabulary

1. **convenient** [kənˈvinjənt] adj.方便的；便利的——helpful; easily used

   *The bus stops right in front of our door, which is very convenient.*

2. **straight edge** [stret] [ɛdʒ] adj.刮鬍刀片的

3. **shoe shine** [ʃu] [ʃaɪn] n.鞋油—— cleaning shoes, especially leather, so they shine

   *My shoes need a shoe shine about once a month.*

4. **deliver** [ dɪ'lɪvɚ ] v.傳送；運送— to give or transport; take something to some place

*The newspapers are delivered after 8 a.m.*

**Dialogs**

---

## 2. Babysitting

*A guest calls Housekeeping.*

A: Good morning. Housekeeping.

B: Hello. I wanted to know, does the hotel offer a babysitting service?

A: Yes, we do, ma'am.

B: Do they have experience?

A: Yes, ma'am. They are experienced and reliable.

B: How much does it cost?

A: NT$50 an hour, with a minimum of 2 hours.

B: That sounds all right.

A: How many children do you have and what are their ages?

B: Two children, aged three and five.

A: When would you like this service, ma'am?

B: From 12:00 to 4:00.

A: And which room are you staying in?

B: Room 4684.

A: Yes, ma'am. We'll send a babysitter to your room just before 12:00. And that's room 4684.

B: That's right. Thank you.

A: You're welcome. Have a nice day.

# Vocabulary

1. **experience** [ɪkˈspɪrɪəns] n.經驗—knowledge, training and/or practice in something

   *This teacher has seven years experience in teaching math.*

2. **reliable** [rɪˈlaɪəbl̩] adj.可靠的— stable; trustworthy; dependable

   *I have known him for ten years and he is very good and reliable.*

3. **minimum** [ˈmɪnəməm] n.最小數— the least amount; not less than; the smallest

   *It will cost at least NT$200 to eat here; that is the minimum.*

# Dialogs

## 3. Laundry

*A guest calls Housekeeping.*

A: Good evening. Housekeeping.

B: Hello. This hotel does have laundry service, doesn't it?

A: Yes, we do.

B: How long does it take?

A: If you leave your laundry out before 10 a.m., we can return it the same day by 7 p.m.

B: I'll need my clothes back before then.

A: Then may I suggest our express laundry service? We can return your laundry in 5 hours at a 50% extra charge.

B: Okay.  And you offer dry cleaning, right?

A: Yes, sir. If you look in your dresser drawer, you'll find laundry forms. Fill in the forms with the important details, put your laundry in the laundry bag, and leave the bag outside your door or on the door handle and we'll pick it up.

B: Do you have a tailor?  One of my buttons came off.

A: Our laundry service can do simple mending.

B: Okay.  I guess that's all.

A: We're happy to be of service to you, sir.  Good night.

## Vocabulary

1. **express** [ɪkˈsprɛs] adj.快的；直達的— fast; quick; direct

*An express letter will arrive in one day.*

2. **extra** [ˈɛkstrə] adj.額外的— spare; further; in addition to

   *It will cost NT$20 extra if the taxi driver helps with our luggage.*

3. **detail** [ˈditel] n.細節— item; small part

   *To understand the painting fully, you must look closely at the details.*

4. **handle** [ˈhændl̩] n.把手— a knob which is moved by the hand to open a door

   *If the door is locked, you cannot move the handle.*

5. **stain** [sten] n.污點— blot; mark; spot; discoloration

   *If a pen's ink gets on clothing, it can leave a very bad stain.*

6. **tailor** [ˈtelɚ] n.裁縫師— person who makes or repairs clothing

   *This tailor makes very fine clothes.*

7. **button** [ˈbʌtn̩] n.—鈕扣

   *Can you help me with this button that fell off my shirt?*

8. **mending** [ˈmɛndɪŋ] n., v.修補— to repair; to fix; to correct

   *The tailor is now mending one of our guest's suits.*

**Exercises** ────────────

## ▸▸ *I. Complete the Dialogs* ◂◂

### 1. Convenient Services

> *A guest calls Housekeeping.*

A: Good afternoon. _____.

B: Hello. I just came from the airport and I have a meeting in a few hours. Do you have any razors?

A: We don't have electric razors, but _____

_____.

B: That's fine. And how about hair dryers?

A: Yes, sir. _____.

B: Good, good. Let me see. Anything else. Oh, yes. What about a shoe shine service?

A: Our hotel _____

_____. We can pick up _____

_____.

B: That's fine.

A: _____, sir?

B: No, that'll be all for now.

A: _____ right away.

B: Thank you.

A: You're welcome, sir. _____.

## 2. Babysitting

*A guest calls Housekeeping.*

A: Good morning. _____.

B: Hello. I wanted to know, does the hotel offer a babysitting service?

A: Yes, we do, ma'am.

B: Do they have experience?

A: Yes, ma'am. _____.

B: How much does it cost?

A: NT$50 an hour, _____ 2 hours.

B: That sounds fine.

A: How _____?

B: One child, age four.

A: When _____?

B: From 12:00 to 4:00.

A: _____?

B: Room 4684.

A: Yes, ma'am.  We'll send _____

_____.  And that's _____.

B: That's right.  Thank you.

A: You're welcome.  _____.

### 3. Laundry

*A guest calls Housekeeping.*

A: Good evening.  Housekeeping.

B: Hello.  Does this hotel have laundry service?

A: Yes, _____.

B: How long does it take?

A: If you _____

_____.

B: I'll need my clothes back before then.

A: Then may I _____? We can

return your_____.

B: Okay.  And you offer dry cleaning, right?

A: Yes, sir.  If you look in _____

_____. Fill in the forms_____

_____

_____

_____.

B: Can your laundry get coffee stains out?

A: We'll _____.

B: Okay. And do you have a tailor? One of my buttons
came off.

A: Our laundry _____.

B: Okay.  I guess that's all.

A: We're happy _____.

## ▸▸ *II. Classroom Role Plays* ◂◂

1. Convenient Services

   A: The guest, Mr. Stilwell, calls Housekeeping to ask about some services.

   B: Staff: Explain the services to the guest.

2. Babysitting

   A: A guest calls Housekeeping to ask about the babysitting service.

   B: Staff: Explain the service to the guest.

3. Laundry

   A: The guest, Mr. Billins, calls Housekeeping to ask about the laundry services.

   B: Staff: Explain the laundry services to the guest.

## ▸▸ *III. Fill in the blanks with the following verbs:* ◂◂

| | | | | |
|---|---|---|---|---|
| send | offer | return | take | get |
| have | pick up | to be | deliver | |

1. We can _____ your laundry by 7 p.m.

2. Yes, sir. We'll _____ someone right away.

3. Can your laundry _____ coffee stains out?

4. We're happy _____ of service to you, ma'am.

5. Our hotel _____ a complimentary shoe shine service.

6. Do your housekeepers _____ experience?

7. How long will it _____ to get my clothes clean?

8. We can _____ your dirty clothes when we. _____
   the hair dryer.

## — ▸▸ *IV. Unscramble the Following Sentences* ◂◂ —

1. look dresser if you'll forms find in you laundry your
   drawers , .

   _____

2. we'll a room your before send 10:00 just to babysitter .

_____

3. ma'am we try but our we'll anything can't best guarantee , , .

_____

4. charge we an laundry have extra at 50% a service express .

_____

5. service your get can out laundry stains coffee ?

_____

## ▸▸ V. Your hotel ◂◂

1. What amenities are offered in your guest bathrooms?

_____   _____

_____   _____

_____   _____

2. What amenities are offered in your guest rooms?

_____   _____

_____   _____

_____   _____


3. What special services does your hotel offer (for example
   — shoe shine) ?

_____   _____

_____   _____

_____   _____


4. What services in your hotel are:

   A) Complimentary          B) Charge for use, and how
                                much?

_____   _____

_____   _____

_____   _____

_____   _____

_____   _____

# *Part IV : Hotel Shopping*

# Unit 11

## Various Items

### 1. Books and Stamps

A: Good afternoon, ma'am. May I help you?

B: Yes. I want to mail these 3 postcards and this letter.

A: The postcards will cost NT$11 each. May I weigh your letter please?

B: Yes.

A: To which country are you sending this letter, ma'am?

B: Germany.

A: The letter will cost NT$15. Altogether NT$48.

B: Here you are. Where can I mail these?

A: Right here, ma'am. I can put the stamps on for you and mail them for you.

B: Thank you very much. Goodbye.

A: You're welcome. Have a nice day.

.............................. *     *     *     * ..............................

A: Good evening, sir. May I help you?

B: Yes. Do you have today's copy of **The Wall Street Journal** and a recent issue of **Time** magazine?

A: I'm sorry, sir. We receive all foreign newspapers one day late, so we have yesterday's issues. We do have this week's *Time*.

B: I suppose yesterday's issue will be all right.  How much is it for one paper and one magazine?

A: A total of NT$150.

B: Okay.  Here's 200.

A: Your change is $50, sir.

B: Thanks, and goodbye.

A: You're welcome, sir.  Have a nice day.

## Vocabulary

1. **mail** [mel] n., v.郵件— letters and packages sent by post; the act of sending

   *If I mail this letter today, it should arrive in 3 days.*

2. **postcard** [`post,kard] n.明信片— small cards sent as mail, like short letters

   *Whenever I travel, I like to send postcards to friends and family.*

3. **letter** [`lɛtə] n.信

   *Sending a letter from Taiwan to America costs about*

—245—

*NT$15.*

4. **weigh** [we] v.重量— to find how heavy something is

   *The more you eat, the more you weigh.*

5. **country** [ˈkʌntrɪ] n.國家— nation; homeland; place of a

   certain people and area

   *Russia is the largest country in the world, while Canada*

   *is second.*

6. **Germany** [ˈdʒɜˈmənɪ] n.德國

   *Germany is a strong country next to France.*

7. **stamp** [stæmp] n.郵票— a paper or mark put on a thing

   to show money has been paid; small paper placed on a

   letter to send through the mail

   *You must put a NT$15 stamp on this letter if you want it*

   *to go to America.*

8. **copy** [ˈkɑpɪ] n., v.複製— something which is the same as

   another

   *The boy delivers 50 copies of the English newspaper to*

   *us every day.*

9. **issue** [ˈɪʃʊ] n.（報刊）期號— copy; edition; a certain copy

   marked by date and/or number

   *This is an old issue of Newsweek.*

10. **recent** [ˈrisn̩t] adj.新近的— not long ago; near in time

    *To get the most recent news, I listen to the radio.*

11. **magazine** [ˌmægəˈzin] n.雜誌

    **Time** *and* **Newsweek** *are two of the most popular news magazines.*

12. **receive** [rɪˈsiv] v.收到— to get; to obtain

    *I receive two magazines by mail.*

# Dialogs

## 2. Jewelry

B: Hello? Is the stone in this necklace an emerald?

A: It's green jade, ma'am.

B: Where does this jade bracelet come from?

A: It's from Australia.

B: And what kind of stone is this?

A: That's a ruby.

B: Is this necklace real gold?

A: No, it's imitation gold.

B: Look at these nice pieces. I really like this one. Where is this jewelry made?

A: It's made in Hong Kong, ma'am.

B: Is this gold ring 18 karat or 24 karat?

A: It is imitation gold.

B: Are the tiny stones in it real diamonds?

A: No, they are imitation diamonds.

B: Where was it made?

A: It was made by hand here in Taiwan.

# Vocabulary

1. **necklace** [ˈnɛklɪs] n.項鍊— jewelry worn as a string around the neck

   *My wife has three gold necklaces.*

2. **emerald** [ˈɛmərəld] n.翡翠— a green precious stone

   *This ring has a beautiful, large emerald.*

3. **jade** [dʒed] n.翡翠；玉

   *The people of Asia are very fond of jade jewelry.*

4. **bracelet** [ˈbreslɪt] n.手鐲— a ring worn around the arm or wrist

   *The bracelet on her arm is silver with jade stones.*

5. **Australia** [ɔˈstreljə] n.澳大利亞

   *Australia is a huge country with few people.*

6. **ruby** [ˈrubɪ] n.紅寶石— a red precious stone

   *Rubies are a favorite stone used in rings and necklaces.*

7. **gold** [gold] n.黃金— a precious yellow metal

   *Most people would like to have more gold.*

8. **imitation** [ˌɪməˈteʃən] adj.仿造的— not real; not true; a copy

   *These rubies are so cheap they must be imitation.*

9. **jewelry** [ˈdʒuəlrɪ] n.珠寶— things made of precious metal

and stones made for wearing

*Most women like to wear jewelry.*

10. **Hong Kong** [hʌŋ] [kʌŋ] n.香港

11. **karat** [ˈkærət] n.克拉

*This jewelry is made from 18 karat gold.*

12. **ring** [rɪŋ] n.戒指— a round band, usually of metal, worn around the finger

*Most married Western men and women wear wedding rings.*

13. **diamond** [ˈdaɪəmənd] n.鑽石— a clear, very hard, very precious stone

*Jewelers like to tell us that diamonds are forever.*

14. **made by hand** 手工

*I only want jewelry that has been made by hand.*

# Dialogs

## 3. Cloisonne Ballpoint Pens

B: Excuse me. Could you tell me about these ballpoint pens?

A: These ballpoint pens are made of cloisonne, which is a special product of Beijing, capital of mainland China. We have 3 colors, gold, silver and blue, and there are 2 styles, one smooth and one rough. The ink core can be replaced. These pens come in attractive boxes and are very popular for personal use and as gifts.

B: Are they all the same price?

A: No, ma'am. The prices are listed here on the boxes.

B: May I see this one?

A: Certainly.

B: May I try writing with it?

A: Of course. Here's a piece of paper.

B: Oh, I like this. Do I pay you here?

A: No, ma'am. Please take these sales slips and pay at the

cashier desk in the corridor.

(Customer returns with receipt.)

A: Thank you, ma'am. Here's your pen. Have a nice day.

## Vocabulary

1. **cloisonne** [klɔɪzəne] n. 景泰藍瓷器

   *Cloisonne products can now be found all over the world.*

2. **ballpoint pen** [ˈbɔlˌpɔɪnt] [pɛn] n. 原子筆

   *May I use your ballpoint pen to write a letter?*

3. **silver** [ˈsɪlvɚ] n.銀— a shiny, gray precious metal

   *Most of my rings are made of silver, though I have two of gold.*

4. **style** [staɪl] n.風格；樣式— kind; sort; type

   *My grandfather only likes to wear old style clothes.*

5. **smooth** [smuð] adj.平滑的— even, flat; not rough

   *Most babies have very smooth skin.*

7. **rough** [rʌf] adj.粗糙的— not smooth; uneven; crude

   *When he is angry, his voice gets very rough.*

8. **ink core** [ɪŋk] [kor] n.筆心

*This pen has a leaking ink core, so I need to get a new one.*

9. **replace** [rɪˈples] v.取代；代替— to change; to take the place of; to restore

   *This letter paper has gotten dirty, so we must replace it.*

10. **attractive** [əˈtræktɪv] adj.引人注意的— pretty; handsome

    *All our hotel staff should keep an attractive appearance.*

11. **popular** [ˈpɑpjələ] adj.受歡迎的— what many people like

    *Steak is the most popular dish in our restaurant.*

12. **personal** [ˈpɜsn̩l] adj.私人的— relating to a person; private; used by oneself

    *This is a personal letter, so no one else should read it.*

## Dialogs

### 4. Foods

B: Good morning.

A: Good morning, sir. May I help you?

B: Yes. I would like to buy this candy bar.

A: This chocolate bar, sir?

B: Yes, and some Chinese tea as a gift. What do you recommend?

A: Most of our tea is a kind of Oulong tea from the high mountains of Taiwan. This tea is very popular here and you can find it used in most tea shops.

B: How do I serve this tea?

A: Use a small teapot. First, warm up the tea pot with hot water. Pour the water out and add tea leaves until the tea pot is one quarter full. Then fill up the tea pot with hot water and immediately pour out again. This serves to rinse the tea. Then pour in more hot water and wait a few minutes before drinking. The same tea leaves can be used several times with the same color, aroma and taste.

B: It sounds very good. How much does it cost ?

A: These boxes are NT$700, these are 1000, and these are 1500.

B: Please give me 3 of these boxes. Can you wrap them for me?

A: Yes, sir. That will be NT$3000 for the tea and 50 for the chocolate, 3050 altogether. Please take these sales slips and pay at the cashier desk in the corridor.

(Customer returns with receipt.)

A: Here you are, sir.

B: Thank you very much.

A: You're welcome, sir. Please visit us again.

## Vocabulary

1. **teapot** [ˈtiˌpɑt] n.茶壺

   *I would like to buy two of these beautiful brown teapots.*

2. **immediately** [ɪˈmidɪɪtlɪ] adv.立刻地— at once; presently; right away

   *These letters are important; please send them immediately.*

3. **rinse** [rɪns] v.沖洗— to clean quickly with water

   *Please rinse the teapot and tea leaves before making the tea.*

4. **aroma** [əˈromə] n.芳香；風味— smell; odor; scent; fragrance

   *These flowers have a wonderful aroma.*

5. **wrap** [ræp] v.包— to cover, usually with paper or plastic

   *These are gifts, so please wrap them with colored paper.*

 **Exercises** ────────────

## ▸▸ *I. Complete the Dialogs* ◂◂

### 1. Books and Stamps

A: Good afternoon, ma'am. _____?

B: Yes. I want to mail these 5 postcards and these two

　letters.

A: _____. May I weigh

　your letters, please?

B: Yes.

A: _____?

B: Germany.

A: _____ NT$15.  Altogether _____.

B: Here you are.  Where can I mail these?

A: Right here, ma'am. _____

　_____.

B: Thank you very much.  Goodbye.

A: _____.

·························· *     *     *      * ··························

A: Good evening, ma'am. _____?

B: Yes. Do you have today's copy of **The Wall Street Journal** and a recent issue of **Time** magazine?

A: I'm sorry, ma'am. _____

_____, so we have yesterday's issues. We do have this week's **Time**.

B: I suppose yesterday's issue will be all right. How much is it for one paper and one magazine?

A: A total of NT$150.

B: Okay. Here's 200.

A: _____.

B: Thanks, and goodbye.

A: You're welcome. _____.

## 2. Cloisonne Ballpoint Pens

B: Excuse me. Could you tell me about these ballpoint pens?

A: _____

_____.

We have 3 colors, gold, silver and blue, and there are 2

styles, one smooth and one rough . The ink core_____

_____. These pens come in attractive boxes

and _____.

B: Are they all the same price?

A: No, ma'am. _____.

B: May I see this one?

A: _____ .

B: May I try writing with it?

A: _____.

B: Oh, I like this.  Do I pay you here?

A: No, ma'am. _____

_____,

(Customer returns with receipt.)

A: Thank you, ma'am. _____.

_____.

## 3. Foods

B: Good morning.

A: Good morning, sir. _____?

B: Yes. I would like to buy some Chinese tea as a gift. What do you recommend?

A: Most of our tea is _____

_____. _____

_____.

B: How do I serve this tea?

A: _____

_____

_____

_____

_____

_____

_____

B: It sounds very good. How much does it cost ?

A: _____.

B: Please give me 3 of these NT$1000 boxes. Can you wrap them for me?

A: Yes, sir. That will be NT$3050 , altogether. _____

_____

_____.

(Customer returns with receipt.)

A: _____.

B: Thank you very much.

A: _____. Please visit us again.

## ▶ *II. Classroom Role Plays* ◀

1. Books and Stamps

   B: You are a guest, Mr. Griffith, wanting to buy some stamps and a magazine.

   A: As the staff member, help the guest with his purchase.

2. Jewelry

   B: You are a guest, Ms. Packard, looking at jewelry.

   A: As the staff member, help the guest with her selection.

3. Cloisonne Ballpoint Pen

    B: You are a guest, Mr. Dole, looking at the cloisonne products.

    A: As the staff member, help the guest with his purchase.

4. Foods

    B: You are a guest, Mrs. Shriver, wanting to buy some chocolate and tea.

    A: As the staff member, help the guest with her selection.

## ▸▸ III. Fill in the blanks with the following verbs: ◂◂

| put | come | take | cost | pay | replaced | wrap |
| receive | made | sending | recommend |

1. We _____ all foreign newspapers one day late.

2. Stamps for the letter will _____ NT$15, sir.

3. Where does this necklace _____ from?

4. These pens are _____ of cloisonne.

5. The ink core of this pen can be _____.

6. What kind of tea do you _____?

7. To which country are you _____ this letter, ma'am?

8. Please _____ these sales slips and _____ at the cashier desk.

9. I can _____ the stamps on for you, sir.

10. Can you _____ these boxes for me?

— ▸▸ *IV. Unscramble the Following Sentences* ◂◂ —

1. weigh may letter please I your , ?

   _____

2. real this or is imitation a this emerald an stone ?

   _____

3. surface one a has one a smooth rough and hassurface.

   _____

4. popular well known China is in tea other this countries and in very .

   _____

5. you what Chinese kind tea of recommend do ?

   _____

# Unit 12

# Textiles and Hotel Policies

## Dialogs

### 1. Silk Shop

A: Good morning.

B: Good morning. How are you today?

A: Fine, thank you. How are you?

B: Fine, thanks.

A: May I help you?

B: Yes. I'm looking for some tablecloths.

A: We have several tablecloths, sir. We have 2 styles, square and round, and they come in small, medium and large sizes.

B: I would like a square one.

A: These are our square ones, sir. We have 2 designs, one with flowers and birds, and the other has a traditional Chinese home. Would you like to look through them, sir?

B: Yes. Could you show me one of each?

A: Yes, sir. Here is one with flowers and birds, and here is one with a traditional home. How do you like them?

B: They are very nice. Is this material silk?

A: No, sir, it's made of rayon and easy to wash.

B: That's good. It looks nice. I'll take the flower and bird design, medium size.

A: Would you like to pay by cash or credit card?

B: I'll pay cash.

A: Yes, sir. Please take these sales slips and pay at the cashier desk in the corridor.

............................. * * * * .................................

A: Good morning. May I help you?

B: Hello. I would like to buy some silk material.

A: Yes, ma'am. We have a wide selection of silk. This silk costs NT$300 per meter and this silk costs NT$350 per meter.

B: I want to make 2 shirts. How much silk do I need?

A: For 2 shirts you will need about 3 meters.

B: Then I'll take 3 meters of this blue one.

## Vocabulary

1. **tablecloth** [`tebḷˌklɔθ] n.桌布— a cloth covering used over tables

   *I like tablecloths with fruit or vegetable designs.*

2. **design** [dɪˈzaɪn] n.花紋；圖案— a pattern, depiction, or illustration

*This tablecloth has a beautiful flower design.*

3. **material** [məˈtɪrɪəl] n.材料— what something is made from; cloth; fabric

*This shirt is made from silk material.*

4. **rayon** [ˈreɑn] n.人造纖維— a shiny man-made material that is very much like silk

*These clothes look like silk, but they are really rayon.*

# Dialogs

## 2. Fashion Wear

A: Good afternoon, sir. May I help you?

B: Good afternoon. I'm looking for a nice shirt, either silk or cotton.

A: This way, please, sir. We have several kinds of shirts. How do you like this one, made of silk?

B: It's very nice, but I don't like the color.

A: What color would you like?

B: Purple.

A: Here you are, sir. Would you like to try this one on?

B: Yes.

A: The fitting room is right over there.

(Guest comes out from the fitting room.)

B: How does it look?

A: It looks a little small for you, sir. I'll get you a larger one.

B: Thank you.

A: Here you are.

(Guest changes shirts.)

A: How does it feel, sir?

B: It fits very well.

A: It looks good on you.

B: I'll take it.

A: Would you like anything else?

B: No.

A: That will be NT$500, sir. Please take these sales slips and pay at the cashier desk in the corridor.

(Customer returns with receipt.)

A: Here you are, sir.  Have a nice  day.

B: Thank you. Goodbye.

··············· *     *     *     * ···············

A: Good evening, ma'am.  May I help you?

B: Hello. This suit looks very nice. Do you have one in size 8?

A: Yes, right here. I'll take it down for you. Here you are. This shirt is silk. It's the latest fashion and the colors are beautiful.  Would you like to try it on?

B: Yes, I would.

A: The fitting room is right over there, ma'am.

(Customer tries it on and returns.)

A: How does it feel?

B: It feels fine.

A: It looks good on you.

B: How much does it cost?

A: NT$2000.

B: I'll take it.

A: Would you like anything else?

B: No, thank you.

A: Please take these sales slips and pay at the cashier desk in the corridor.

(Customer returns with receipt.)

A: Thank you, ma'am. Here's your suit. Have a nice day.

## Vocabulary

1. **fashion** [ˈfæʃən] n.流行款式— the popular style of a time

   *This suit was very fashionable about 20 years ago.*

2. **fitting room** [ˈfɪtɪŋ][rum] n.試衣室— room for trying on clothes

   *Our clothes shop has two fitting rooms, one for men and the other for women.*

3. **fit** [fɪt] n., v.適合；合身— to be correctly shaped for; the right size

   *I really like these shoes, but they don't fit, so I won't buy them.*

4. **suit** [sut] n.（一套）衣服— a set of clothes; a matching outfit

   *Most businessmen like to wear dark suits.*

# Dialogs

## 3. Refusing Suitors

> *In the clothing shop, a customer comes up to one of the staff.*

B: Excuse me, miss?

A: Yes, sir. May I help you?

B: While I was walking by, I looked in and saw you and thought, "What is a beautiful girl like her doing working here?"

A: Just working, sir. Is there anything you'd like to buy?

B: Maybe. Maybe. May I ask you a question?

A: Certainly.

B: Are you married?

A: What, sir? What does that have to do—

B: Nothing. Nothing. I just meant, a beautiful girl like you must have several boyfriends.

A: Thank you for your kind compliment, sir, but—

B: Well, can I ask you out for dinner?

A: I'm sorry, sir, but it's hotel policy that staff cannot accept guests' invitations for a date.

B: That's no problem. We don't have to go to a restaurant in this hotel. After you get off work, we can go to any restaurant you like.

A: I'm sorry, sir.

B: It's just that you're so beautiful.

A: Thank you, sir, but I really can't.

B: Are you sure?

A: Yes, I'm sorry, but it is our policy.

B: Oh, just this once!

A: If you like, I can call the management to talk with you.

B: All right, all right, I'm going.

# Vocabulary

1. **married** [ˋmærɪd] v.已婚的— to have a husband or wife

   *My wife and I have been married for nine years.*

2. **compliment** [ˋkɑmpləmənt] n.讚美；問候— spoken praise; to honor; a flattering remark

   *If the waitress is very good, I will compliment her.*

3. **policy** [ˋpɑləsɪ] n.政策；方針— rules; a method of action selected by a company

   *Our restaurant policy is that all workers must regularly wash their hands.*

4. **accept** [əkˋsɛpt] v.接受— receive; welcome; take; to say yes

   *When he asked her to marry him, she accepted.*

5. **invitation** [͵ɪnvəˋteʃən] n.邀請— to ask or request something

   *I gave her an invitation to come to my birthday party.*

6. **date** [det] n., v.約會— a meeting between people set at a certain time, especially between a man and a woman for romantic purposes

   *My boyfriend and I have been dating for five months, now.*

# Dialogs

## 4. One Price Policy

*A guest enters the art shop.*

A: Good evening, sir. May I help you?

B: Yes. I'm looking for a traditional Chinese painting and I noticed you have many, here.

A: Yes, we do, sir. We have several by well known local artists.

B: I'd like a landscape with mountains and rivers.

A: How about this one, sir? Or this one over here?

B: Oh, yes. They're both nice. This one even has two little people in it.

A: This is a very old and popular style of painting.

B: How much is it?

A: NT$10,000.

B: That much?

A: Yes, sir. The artist is well known and, as you can see, it is a very fine painting.

B: I understand, but that still seems like quite a high price. I do like it, though. Tell you what, I'll offer you 7,000 for it.

A: I'm sorry, sir, but our hotel has a one price policy. We are not allowed to bargain.

B: Oh, well, then I'll have to think about it.

A: Please do look around the shop and if you need anything,

I'll be here to help.

## Vocabulary

1. **notice** [ˋnotɪs] v.注意— to see; to make note of; to become aware of

   *Did you notice the beautiful painting hanging by the door?*

2. **landscape** [ˋlænd͵skep] n.風景— a picture showing natural scenery

   *Chinese traditional landscape painting usually has mountains and water.*

3. **bargain** [ˋbargɪn] n., v.協議；買賣— argue over price; to deal or come to an agreement about money

   *When I shop, I always try to bargain for a lower price.*

**Note: In refusing suitors, one of the best and easiest methods is to simply say, "I'm married."**

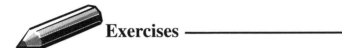

**Exercises** ———————————————————

## ▸▸ *I. Complete the dialogs* ◂◂

### 1. Fashion Wear

A: Good afternoon, sir. _____?

B: Good afternoon.  I'm looking for a nice shirt.

A: This way, please, sir. _____.

_____?

B: It's very nice, but I don't like the color.

A: _____?

B: Green.

A: Here you are, sir. _____?

B: Yes.

A: _____.

   (Guest comes out from the fitting room.)

B: How does it look?

A: It looks a little small for you, sir. _____

_____.

B: Thank you.

A: Here you are.

   (Customer changes shirts.)

A: _____?

B: It fits very well.

A: It looks good on you.

B: I'll take it.

A: _____?

B: No.

A: That will be NT$300, sir. _____

   _____,

   (Customer returns with receipt.)

A: Here you are, sir. _____.

B: Thank you. Goodbye.


.............................. *       *       *       * ..............................


A: Good evening, ma'am. _____?

B: Hello. This suit looks very nice.  Do you have one in size
   10?

−280−

A: Yes, here is one. I'll take it down for you. Here you are. This shirt is silk. It's the latest fashion and the colors are beautiful. _____?

B: Yes, I would.

A: _____.

(Customer tries it on and returns.)

A: _____?

B: It feels fine.

A: _____.

B: How much does it cost?

A: NT$1000.

B: I'll take it.

A: _____?

B: No, thank you.

A: _____

_____.

(Customer returns with receipt.)

A: Thank you, ma'am. _____. _____

_____.

## 2. Silk Shop

A: Good morning.

B: Good morning.  How are you today?

A: _____._____?

B: Fine, thanks.

A: _____?

B: Yes.  I'm looking for some tablecloths.

A: We have several tablecloths, sir.  We have 2 styles,_____

_____.

B: I would like a square one.

A: _____.  We have 2 designs,

one with flowers and birds, and the other has a traditional

Chinese home. _____

_____?

B: Yes. Could you show me one of each?

A: Yes, sir.  Here is one _____, __

_____.  How

do you like them?

B: They are very nice.  Is this material silk?

A: _____.

B: That's good. It looks nice. I'll take this one in a large

size.

A: _____?

B: I'll pay cash.

A: _____

_____.

........................... *     *     *     * .............................

A: _____?

B: Hello.  I would like to buy some silk.

A: Yes,  ma'am. _____. _____

_____.

B: I want to make 4 shirts.  How much silk do I need?

A: _____.

B: I'll take 6 meters of the blue one.

## 3. Refusing Suitors

*In the clothing shop, a guest comes up to one of the staff.*

B: Excuse me, miss?

A: Yes, sir. _____?

B: While I was walking by, I looked in and saw you and thought, "What is a beautiful girl like her doing working here?"

A: Just working, sir. _____?

B: Maybe. Maybe. May I ask you a question?

A: Certainly.

B: Are you married?

A: What, sir? What does that have to do—

B: Nothing. Nothing. I just meant, a beautiful girl like you must have several boyfriends.

A: _____,

   but—

B: Well, can I ask you out for dinner?

A: I'm sorry, sir, but _____

_____.

B: That's no problem. We don't have to go to a restaurant in this hotel. After you get off work, we can go to any restaurant you like.

A: _____.

B: It's just that you're so beautiful.

A: Thank you, sir, _____.

## 4. One Price Policy

*A guest enters the art shop.*

A: Good evening, sir. _____?

B: Yes. I'm looking for a traditional Chinese painting and I noticed you have many, here.

A: Yes, we do, sir. _____.

B: I'd like a landscape with mountains and rivers.

A: _____? Or this one over here?

B: Oh, yes. They're both nice. This one even has two little people in it.

A: This is a very old and _____.

B: How much is it?

A: NT$7000.

B: That much?

A: Yes, sir. The artist is well known and, _____
_____.

B: I understand, but that still seems like quite a high price. I do like it, though. Tell you what, I'll offer you 5000 dollars for it.

A: I'm sorry, sir, but _____. We are not allowed to bargain.

B: Oh, well, I'll have to think about it.

A: Please do look around the shop and _____
_____.

———————— ▸▸ *II. Role Plays* ◂◂ ————————

1. Refusing a Suitor

    B: As the guest, you are interested in asking one of the staff out on a date.

    A: Politely refuse your suitor.

2. One Price Policy

    B: As a guest, you enter the art shop and want to buy a painting, but you think the price is too high, so you try bargaining with the sales staff.

    A: Help the guest choose a painting, and politely explain the hotel's one price policy.

3. Silk Shop

    B: You are interested in buying some silk items.

    A: Help the customer make a good selection.

4. Fashion Wear Shop

    B: You want to buy some nice clothing.

    A: Help the customer make a good choice.

## ▸▸ III. Match the Following Sentences ◂◂

_____ 1. The fitting room is

_____ 2. For 2 shirts you will need

_____ 3. In our shop, we have

_____ 4. You can pay

_____ 5. This suit looks

_____ 6. All of our clothes are

_____ 7. Hotel policy states that staff cannot accept

_____ 8. I think this painting is

A. about 3 meters.

B. very nice on you.

C. very expensive.

D. right over there.

E. guests' invitations for a date.

F. by cash or credit card.

G. the latest fashion.

H. a wide selection of silk.

———————— ▸▸ *IV. Multiple Choice* ◂◂ ————————

1. If a guest is interested in some clothing or art in your shop, you should _____.

   a. ask the guest how much he/she wants to spend

   b. offer to help the guest look through the selection

   c. let the guest look where he/she wants

   d. tell the guest that the more expensive items are better

2. If a guest looks at and likes a piece of clothing , you should _____.

   a. ask him/her to buy it at the cashier's desk

   b. ask the guest to pay you for it

   c. say how good it would look on him/her

   d. ask the guest to try it on

3. If a guest continues to ask you for a date, you should____.

   a. thank him/her, and repeat the hotel policy

   b. compliment the guest

   c. call the hotel security

   d. ask the guest to leave

4. If a guest offers a lower price for a product, you should

    _____.

    a. start bargaining with the guest

    b. ask the guest to leave

    c. call the Assistant Manager

    d. tell the guest that the hotel has a one price policy

## ▸▸ V. Your Hotel ◂◂

1. Does your hotel have a one price policy?

    _____

    _____

2. What is your hotel's policy on dating?

    _____

    _____

3. Does your hotel have an art shop? What kinds of art, styles of paintings, and which well-known artists are represented?

    _____

    _____

# Unit 13

# Arts and Crafts

## Dialogs

### 1. Carpet Center

A: Good morning, sir.  May I help you?

B: Good morning. I would like to buy a carpet.

A: Yes, sir. We have silk carpets, rayon, and woolen carpets in a wide range of sizes and designs.

B: Where are these carpets made ?

A: These are made in mainland China, while these are Middle Eastern.

B: How long does it take to make one of these carpets?

A: One carpet takes about 6 months.

B: I would like to buy an 8x10 carpet with a traditional Chinese design.

A: These carpets are 8x10 and there are many different designs.  How do you like this one ?

B: I like it very much. Oh... and this one over here is very nice. How much is it?

A: It is NT$6500.

B: Do you have a forwarding service? Can you ship it to Seattle for me?

A: We can send it for you by air or by sea. Air shipments are charged by weight. Sea shipments are charged by volume. This is a large wool carpet. I suggest you send it by sea.

B: O.K. How long do sea shipments take?

A: From here to Seattle should take around 2 months.

B: That's all right.

A: Would you fill out this form please, sir?

B: Yes.

A: Please take these sales slips and pay at the cashier desk in the corridor.

   (Customer returns with receipt.)

A: Thank you, sir. We'll be sending your carpet as soon as possible.

B: Thank you.

# Vocabulary

1. **carpet** [ˋkarpɪt] n.地毯— a floor covering made of heavy fabric material

   *Middle Eastern wool carpets are famous all over the world.*

2. **wool** [wʊl] n.毛線— the hair of sheep

   *Wool is a very warm fabric.*

3. **forwarding service** [ˋfɔrwədɪŋ][ˋsɝvɪs] n.運貨服務—a service for sending things by post for a customer

   *Our hotel has a forwarding service to help guests ship their goods home.*

4. **weight** [wet] n.重量— how heavy something is

   *The more I eat, the more my weight goes up.*

5. **volume** [ˋvɑljəm] n.體積— the size of something; the space something takes

   *It is usually cheaper to mail things by volume.*

# Dialogs

## 2. Folk Arts and Crafts Shop

B: Hello.

A: Good afternoon, ma'am.  May I help you?

B: Thank you.  I'm just looking.

A: Yes, ma'am.  If you need my help, please call me.

B: Where was this made?

A: This hanging piece was made in Taitung, southeastern

Taiwan by local craftsmen. It has beautiful tribal features. Do you like it, ma'am?

B: Yes, I do. Is it expensive?

A: No. Only NT$100 each.

B: That's a good bargain. I'll take 10, please. Could you wrap them up for me individually?

A: Yes, ma'am. The total cost is 1000 dollars. Would you like anything else?

B: No, just these. Where do I pay?

A: Please take these sales slips and pay at the cashier desk in the corridor.

(Customer returns with receipt.)

A: Thank you. Have a nice day.

## Vocabulary

1. **folk** [ˋfok] adj., n.通俗的— a group of people forming a tribe; of a tribe

   *I enjoy old folk songs.*

2. **arts and crafts** [ɑrt] [kræft] n.手工藝品

*When I travel, I take home a few arts and craft pieces from local tribes.*

3. **hang** [hæŋ] v.把…掛起— to dangle; to hold or fasten from above

   *Many people hang art on their walls.*

4. **(a) bargain** [ˋbargɪn] n.廉價— a good price; a low price; cheap

   *These shirts were such a bargain, I bought 4 of them.*

5. **individually** [͵ɪndəˋvɪdʒvəlɪ] adv.個別地— made for one person; separate

   *I want these crafts wrapped individually so I can give them to different people.*

# Dialogs

## 3. Seals - Name Chops

*Don Nichols and his girlfriend Nancy Thomas are walking around the hotel shops area when they see the stone seals.*

B: Nancy, look at these.

C: Oh, how interesting! All kinds of little animals carved from... is it stone?

B: I think so. But see, they are all different colors, and the prices vary widely. It must be different kinds of stone. Maybe marble.

A: Good afternoon, ma'am, sir. May I help you?

B: Yes. What are these little stone figures for?

A: They are used to make seals, what some people call "name chops". Carving stone to make seals is a art of traditional China which goes back thousands of years. Many of our foreign guests like to choose a stone and have ourhotel artist carve their Chinese names into the seal.

C: That would be nice, but we don't have Chinese names.

A: That's no problem, ma'am. It is not difficult to translate the sounds of Western names into similar Chinese characters.

C: Don, let's do it.

A: Okay. Which stone do you like?

C: They have a lot of dragons, here.

A: Yes, ma'am. In China, the dragon is a symbol for men.

C: What about women?

A: The phoenix symbolizes women.

C: How about that, Don? You get the dragon, I get the phoenix.

B: Sounds good to me.

A: Would you like your first names or surnames carved on the seals?

C: I think our surnames.

B: Yeah, that would be good.

A: Would you like only the Chinese characters carved, or the Chinese and English lettering together?

C: Mmm, how about both together?

B: Sure.

A: Could you please spell your surnames for me?

B: Hers is T.H.O.M.A.S. Thomas. Mine is N.I.C.H.O.L.S. Nichols.

A: Thank you. The seal carving is done overnight, so you can pick them up tomorrow morning. The stones cost NT$200 each and the carving will be NT$100 each. Altogether, NT$600. Here are the sales slips. You can pay at the cashier desk in the corridor.

........................................................................................................................

## Vocabulary

1. **seal** [sil] n.印章— a stamp or signature
   *Most Chinese seals are made of stone or wood.*

2. **interesting** [ˈɪntərɪstɪŋ] adj.有趣的— pleasing; exciting; attractive
   *Tina thinks love novels are the most interesting.*

3. **carve** [kɑrv] v.雕刻— to cut or slice; to shape by cutting
   *Have you ever carved your name into a tree?*

4. **vary** [ˈvɛrɪ] v.種類— to have a range of difference; to be different
   *Our jewelry varies in price from NT$200 to over NT$30,000.*

5. **widely** [ˈwaɪdlɪ] adv.廣泛地— largely; greatly
   *This singer is widely known, from Hong Kong to New York.*

6. **marble** [ˈmarbl̩] n.大理石
   *Many rich people like to use marble floors in their*

*homes.*

7. **figure** [ˈfɪgjə] n.外型；人物— an image; a design or shape

   *The dragon is an important figure in Chinese culture.*

8. **choose** [tʃuz] v.選擇— to select one over another; to decide on

   *In America, the people choose a president every four years.*

9. **similar** [ˈsɪmələ] adj.相像的— to be alike or related; almost the same

   *These two girls look so similar, I always think they are sisters.*

10. **character (Chinese writing)** [ˈkærɪktə] n.字— a drawn word, letter, mark or symbol

    *Many Chinese characters look like little pictures.*

11. **dragon** [ˈdrægən] n.龍— a fantastic snake-like animal

    *Dragons are usually very bad animals in Western folk stories.*

12. **symbol** [ˈsɪmbl̩] n.記號— a sign or mark to represent something else

    *In China, the dragon was a symbol of the emperor.*

13. **phoenix** [ˈfinɪks] n.鳳凰— a fantastic bird-like animal

*The phoenix is often a symbol for women, while dragons represent men.*

## Exercises

### ▶▶ *I. Complete the Dialogs* ◀◀

| 1. Carpet Center |

A: Good morning, sir. _____?

B: Good morning.  I would like to buy a carpet.

A: Yes, sir. _____, _____

_____.

B: Where are these carpets made ?

A: _____the

Middle East.

B: How long does it take to make one of these carpets?

A: _____about 6 months.

B: I would like to buy an 8 x 12 carpet with a Chinese

design.

A: These carpets are 8 x 12 and there are many different

designs._____?

B: I like it very much.  How much is it ?

A: It is NT$8000.

B: Do you have a forwarding service? Can you ship it to San Francisco for me?

A: _____. Air shipments are charged by weight. _____

_____. _____.

I suggest you send it by sea.

B: O.K. How long do sea shipments take?

A: From here to San Francisco should take around 2 months.

B: That would be all right.

A: _____?

B: Yes.

A: _____.

(Customer returns with receipt.)

A: Thank you, sir. We'll be sending your carpet as soon as possible.

B: Thank you.

## 2. Folk Arts and Crafts Shop

B: Hello.

A: Good afternoon, ma'am. _____?

B: Thank you. I'm just looking.

A: _____.

B: Where was this made?

A: This hanging piece was made in XishuangBanna, Yunnan province, in the far south of China by local craftsmen. It has beautiful local Chinese features. Do you like it, ma'am?

B: Yes, I do. Is it expensive?

A: No. Only NT$300 each.

B: That's a good bargain. I'll take 10, please. Could you wrap them up for me individually?

A: Yes, ma'am. _____. _____

_____?

B: No, just these. Where do I pay?

A: _____.

(Customer returns with receipt.)

A: _____. _____.

## 3. Seals - Name Chops

*Tim Baker and his girlfriend Shirley Lennox are walking around the hotel shops area when they see the stone seals.*

B: Shirley, look at these.

C: Oh, how interesting! All kinds of little animals carved from... is it stone?

B: I think so. But see, they are all different colors, and the prices vary widely. It must be different kinds of stone. Maybe marble.

A: Good afternoon, ma'am, sir. _____?

B: Yes. What are these little stone figures for?

A: _____

_____. Carving stone to make seals is a traditional

_____.

Many of our foreign guests like to choose a stone and

have our hotel artist _____

_____.

C: That would be nice, but we don't have Chinese names.

A: That's no problem, ma'am. _____

_____.

C: Tim, let's do it.

B: Okay. Which stone do you like?

C: They have a lot of dragons, here.

A: Yes, ma'am. In China, _____

_____.

C: What about women?

A: _____.

C: How about that, Tim? You get the dragon, I get the phoenix.

B: Sounds okay to me.

A: Would you like your first names or _____

_____?

C: I think our surnames.

B: Yeah, that sounds good.

A: Would you like only the Chinese characters carved, or

_____?

C: Mmm, how about both together?

B: Sure.

A: _____?

B: Hers is L.E.N.N.O.X. Lennox. Mine is B.A.K.E.R. Baker.

A: Thank you.  The seal carving is done overnight, _____
_____.  The stones cost
NT$250 each and the carving will be $50 each.
Altogether, NT$600. _____

_____

_____


--------- ▸▸ *II. Classroom Role Plays* ◂◂ ---------


1. Seals — Name Chops

   B, C: The guests, John Templeton and his girlfriend Stella
   Li are looking at the stone seals.

   A: Help the guests understand stone seals and make a
   good selection, and explain to them the hotel carving
   service.

2. Folk Arts and Crafts Shop

    B: The guest is looking for some arts and crafts to take home as presents.

    A: Help the guest in choosing gifts.

3. Carpet Center

    B: The guest wants to purchase a silk carpet and send it to New York.

    A: Help the guest in choosing, and explain the hotel's forwarding service.

## ▶▶ III. Fill in the blanks with the ◀◀ appropriate words listed below

| charged | like | buy | fill out |
|---------|------|-----|----------|
| is | made | send | carve | wrap |

1. Where are these carpets _____?

2. I would like to _____ a 9 x 12 carpet with a traditional design.

3. I really _____ this silk design.

4. We can _____ it for you by air or by sea.

5. Could you _____ this up for me?

6. Sea shipments are _____ by volume.

7. Our artist can _____ your names into the seals, if you like.

8. In China, the phoenix _____ a symbol for women.

9. Would you _____ this form, please?

— ►► *IV. Unscramble the Following Sentences.* ◄◄ —

1. Chinese would names but nice that have be don't we .

   _____

2. symbol the China for dragon in a men is .

   _____

3. made and these wool of designs many are carpets there are .

_____

4. send sea it so I this a wool is you by large suggest carpet , .

_____

5. kinds animals all we marble carved of from little have .

_____

# *Part V : Hotel Management*

# Unit 14

# Handling Complaints

### Dialogs

| 1. Coffee Shop Manager |
| --- |

*After a waitress has difficulty with a guest, she calls over the Coffee Shop Manager.*

A: Good afternoon, sir. May I help you?

B: I hope so. I was just telling your waitress that I ordered a pizza with meat and cheese, but no seafood. Now look at this! It's got seafood all over it. And when I told her, she just seemed to ignore me and walked away. Not what I would call 4 star service.

A: I'm very sorry about that, sir. I'm sure our waitress did not mean to be impolite. Our English is quite limited, so we sometimes misunderstand guests' requests.

B: Well, what do we do now? I don't like seafood pizza.

A: Of course we'll change it, sir. And I'll tell the chef, myself, "no seafood".

B: Well, that's better. Next...

A: Yes, sir?

B: This wine seems to be sour.

A: Yes, sir. This particular local white wine does have a fruity, sour taste.

B: Oh. I wish I'd known that before ordering it.

A: Would you like to try another wine?

B: I don't know.

A: Considering the inconvenience we've caused you, sir,

may I offer a dry white wine, on the house?

B: Well, yes.  That would be quite nice. Thank you.

## Vocabulary

1. **ignore** [ɪgˈnor] v.不理會— to not pay attention to; neglect; overlook

   *Do not ignore people or they may become angry.*

2. **limited** [ˈlɪmɪtɪd] v.有限的— poor; finite; restricted

   *These rooms are limited to two guests per room.*

3. **sour** [ˈsaʊr] adj.酸的— tart; acidic; tangy

   *Lemons are famous for being sour.*

4. **particular** [pəˈtɪkjələ] adj.特殊的— specific; certain; special

   *This particular guest always smiles and often laughs.*

5. **on the house** 免費的— free; at no charge; complimentary

   *Because it is your birthday, this cake is on the house.*

# Dialogs

## 2. Loss of Property

*Miss Karras cannot find her purse. She goes to the front desk and is referred to the Assistant Manager.*

A: Hello, ma'am. May I help you?

B: I'm afraid that someone may have stolen my purse.

A: I'm sorry to hear that, ma'am. Would you like for me to contact the police?

B: That's up to you.

A: What do you mean, ma'am?

B: I think it may have been the housekeeper.

A: Did you see her take it, ma'am?

B: No. But the room is where I left it, and now it's not there.

A: I see. We'll certainly do all we can to help you find your purse, ma'am.

B: And if we can't find it?

A: That will be a matter for the police. But first, let us go with a room attendant to look carefully through your room. This way, we can be more certain that your purse was not simply displaced.

B: Displaced? I don't think so. I always leave my purse on top of the desk.

A: We just want to be sure, ma'am. Afterwards, we'll contact the police and have you fill out a Lost Articles form.

B: Okay, okay.

......................................................................................................................

## Vocabulary

1. **purse** [pɝs] n.手提包— handbag; shoulder bag; wallet

   *My wife has a black leather purse which she always carries.*

2. **refer** [rɪˈfɝ] v.交付— to direct; send to; to look into

   *For a list of room service foods, please refer to the room guide.*

3. **steal/stolen** [stil][stolən] v.偷；搶— to rob; to take something without permission

   *When my purse was stolen on the bus, I called the police.*

4. **up to (you)** 給（你）決定— given to; who will decide

   *It is up to you where we eat tonight.*

5. **matter** [ˈmætɚ] n.事情— a thing; a situation; a condition

   *If a guest's money is stolen, this matter must be reported to the manager.*

6. **displace** [dɪsˈples] v.遺失— lose; dislocate

*When I displaced my key, it took me an hour to find it.*

7. **lost articles** [lɔst]['artɪkl̩s] n.遺失的東西— things which cannot be found; displaced items

*Every week we find some guests' lost articles.*

# Dialogs

## 3. Damage Claims

*The Director of Housekeeping is called to a guest's room by another housekeeper.*

A: Good morning, sir. Miss Li, your housekeeper, said there was some problem in your room.

B: Well, yes. I seem to have, uh, knocked over and broken one of your lamps.

A: This is the lamp, sir?

B: Yes. That's the one.

A: It seems to be rather badly damaged. We'll have to replace it with a new one.

B: I really am sorry.

A: I'm afraid, sir, that we'll have to charge this to your room account.

B: How much?

A: About NT$750.

B: So much? That seems rather high.

A: It is a high quality lamp, sir.

B: What will you do with it?

A: This one we have to throw away, unless you want it?

B: No, no, thank you.

A: I'll have a new lamp brought this afternoon for you.

B: All right. Thanks.

A: We're sorry for this trouble, sir. Do enjoy your stay.

### Vocabulary

1. **knock over** [nɑk][ˋovɚ] v.撞倒— overturn; upset

   *When I ran into the chair I knocked it over.*

2. **break/broken** [brek][ˋbrokən] v.打破；毀壞— destroy; damage; hurt

   *If you drop a glass on the floor, you may break it.*

3. **lamp** [læmp] n.燈

4. **damage** [ˋdæmɪdʒ] n., v.損壞；損失— to hurt; harm; destroy; break

   *If you damage something in the hotel, you must pay for it.*

5. **throw away** [θro][əˋwe] v.扔掉— to get rid of; remove; count as waste

   *Every evening we throw away the garbage.*

# Dialogs

## 4. Billing Disagreements

*The Assistant Manager is called over to the check out counter.*

B: Are you the Assistant Manager?

A: Yes, ma'am. May I help you?

B: There are two problems with my bill.

A: I'm sorry about that, ma'am. What are the problems?

B: First, there's a bill here for using the minibar. That's NT$200? I only drank one Coke. How could it possibly be that much?

A: I'm sorry for that mistake, ma'am. Let me change that for you. It should be only $50.

B: Good. That's better.

A: And the second problem?

B: This one, here. A NT$250 charge for a phone call.

A: Did you make any long distance calls during your stay, ma'am?

B: Well, not really. I tried calling my friend in Japan, but my friend wasn't there.

A: Did you talk to anyone?

B: Well, yes. But only for a few seconds. Just long enough to find out my friend wasn't there. Then I hung up the phone.

A: I'm sorry, ma'am, but there's nothing I can do about that. You see, any completed call, no matter how short, incurs a minimum charge. That's set by the hotel and written in the room guide.

B: Oh.

A: I'm sorry for the inconvenience, ma'am. May I be of any further help?

B: No. That's all.

A: Have a pleasant trip home. We hope you've enjoyed your stay.

# Vocabulary

1. **possibly** [ˈpɑsəblɪ] adv.或許— being able; having the ability

   *He could not possibly walk from here to there in ten minutes; he must have taken a taxi.*

2. **long distance** [lɔŋ] [ˈdɪstəns] adj. 長途的

3. **hang/hung up** [hæŋ] v.把⋯掛上

4. **complete** [kəmˈplit] v.完成— finish; end; whole

   *It takes at least one hour to complete this test.*

   *A complete meal with soup, main course, and beverage costs $450.*

5. **incur** [ɪnˈkɝ] v.招致；受— to meet with; bring down upon oneself

   *If you are not polite, you may incur the guests' and the manager's anger.*

**Exercises** ——————————————

## ▶▶ *I. Complete the Dialogs* ◀◀

### 1. Coffee Shop Manager

*After a waitress has difficulty with a guest, she calls over the Coffee Shop Manager.*

A: Good afternoon, sir. _____?

B: I hope so. I was just telling your waitress that I ordered a pizza with meat and cheese, but no seafood. Now look at this! It's got seafood all over it. And when I told her, she just seemed to ignore me and walked away. Not what I would call 4 star service.

A: _____. I'm sure our waitress did not _____.
Our English ability is quite limited, so_____
_____.

—328—

B: Well, what do we do now?  I don't like seafood pizza.

A: _____. And I'll

   tell _____.

B: Well, that's better.  Next...

A: Yes, sir?

B: This wine seems to be sour.

A: Yes, sir.  This _____

   _____.

B: Oh.  I wish I'd known that before ordering it.

A: Would you like _____?

B: I don't know.

A: _____

   _____, may I offer a dry white

   wine, _____?

B: Well, yes.  That would be quite nice.  Thank you.

## 2. Loss of Property

*Miss Cardin cannot find her purse. She goes to the front desk and is referred to the Assistant Manager.*

A: Hello, ma'am. _____?

B: I'm afraid that someone may have stolen my purse.

A: _____. Would you like

　　for me _____?

B: That's up to you.

A: What do you mean, ma'am?

B: I think it may have been the housekeeper.

A: _____?

B: No. But the room is where I left it, and now it's not there.

A: I see. We'll certainly _____

_____.

B: And if we can't find it?

A: That will be a matter for the police. But first, _____

_____

_____. This way, we can be more certain

that _____.

B: Displaced?  I don't think so.  I always leave my purse on

top of the desk.

A: We just _____. Afterwards,

we'll contact the police and _____

_____.

B: Okay, okay.

## 3. Damage Claims

*The Director of Housekeeping is called to a guest's*
*room by another housekeeper.*

A: Good morning, sir.  Miss Li, your housekeeper, _____

_____.

B: Well, yes.  I seem to have, uh, knocked over and broken

one of your lamps.

A: This is the lamp, sir?

B: Yes.  That's the one.

A: It seems to be rather badly damaged.  _____

_____.

B: I really am sorry.

A: I'm afraid, sir, that _____

_____.

B: How much?

A: About NT$850.

B: So much?  That seems rather high.

A: _____.

B: What will you do with it?

A: This one _____?

B: No, no, thank you.

A: I'll have a new _____.

B: All right.  Thanks.

A: We're sorry_____.

## 4. Billing Disagreements

> *The Assistant Manager is called over to the check out counter.*

B: Are you the Assistant Manager?

A: Yes, ma'am. _____?

B: There are two problems with my bill.

A: _____. What are the problems?

B: First, there's a bill here for using the minibar. NT$300 yuan? I only drank one Coke. How could it possibly be that much?

A: _____. Let me _____ _____. It should be only $50.

B: Good. That's better.

A: And the second problem?

B: This one, here. A NT$350 charge for a phone call.

A: _____?

B: Well, not really. I tried calling my friend in Japan, but my friend wasn't there.

A: _____?

B: Well, yes.  But only for a few seconds. Just long enough to find out my friend wasn't there. Then I hung up the phone.

A: I'm sorry, ma'am, but _____

_____. You see, any_____

_____ a minimum

charge.  That's set by _____

_____.

B: Oh.

A: I'm sorry for _____

_____. May I be of any further help?

B: No. That's all.

A: Have a pleasant trip home. _____

_____.

——————— ▸▸ *II. Classroom Role Plays* ◂◂ ———————

1. Coffee Shop Manager

    B: As a hotel guest, you are having some problems with the food.

    A: You are the Coffee Shop Manager. After a waitress has difficulty with a guest, she calls you over to help.

2. Loss of Property

    B: Your name is Mr. Warren, and you cannot find your gold ring. You go to the front desk and are referred to the Assistant Manager.

    A: As Assistant Manager, you must help the guest, and the hotel.

3. Damage Claims

    A: As the Director of Housekeeping, you are called to a guest's room by another housekeeper.

    B: You are the guest, and while smoking, accidentally burned your bed blanket and cover.

4. Billing Disagreements

A: As the Assistant Manager, you are called over to the check out counter.

B: Your name is Rob Narius and you think the hotel has made some mistakes with your bill.

— ▸▸ *III. Make Sentences with the Words Given* ◂◂ —

Example I / waitress / not mean / impolite .

= I'm sure our waitress did not mean to beimpolite.

1. see / housekeeper / take / wallet ?

_____

2. inconvenience / caused you / offer / wine / on the house ?

_____

3. This way we / certain / your wallet / displaced .

_____

4. We / charge / your room .

_____

5. completed call / no matter / minimum charge .

_____

———— ▸▸ *IV. Multiple Choice* ◂◂ ————

1. If a mistake in communication occurs, you should _____.

   a. fault the guest for not speaking clearly

   b. not bother with it

   c. give the guest some free food

   d. apologize and offer to help

2. If a guest cannot find something valuable (wallet, ring, etc.), you should _____.

   a. call a hotel security guard

   b. ask to search the room with the guest

   c. ask the guest to look through his things, again

   d. call the police

3. If a guest breaks something, you should _____.

   a. call the police.

   b. politely ask the guest to leave.

   c. ignore the problem.

   d. politely ask the guest to pay for the broken article.

# Appendix

## Alphabetical Vocabulary List

| Letter | Page | Letter | Page |
|--------|------|--------|------|
| jade 翡翠；玉 | 249 | local 地方性的 | 104 |
| jewelry 珠寶 | 249 | long distance 長途的 | 327 |
| juice 果汁 | 166 | lost articles 遺失的東西 | 321 |
| | | lounge 休息室 | 27 |
| **K** | | luggage 行李 | 22 |
| karat 克拉 | 250 | | |
| kiosk 公共電話亭 | 27 | **M** | |
| knife 刀 | 148 | made by hand 手工 | 250 |
| knock over 撞倒 | 324 | magazine 雜誌 | 247 |
| Korean 韓國的 | 173 | mail 郵件 | 245 |
| | | make up 整理；組織 | 205 |
| **L** | | manager 負責人 | 8 |
| lamp 燈 | 324 | marble 大理石 | 300 |
| landscape 風景 | 278 | married 已婚的 | 275 |
| leak 漏洞 | 84 | material 材料 | 268 |
| leftover 殘留的部分 | 104 | matter 事情 | 320 |
| letter 信 | 245 | Mediterranean 地中海的 | 27 |
| limited 有限的 | 317 | medium-rare 五分熟 | 167 |
| liquor 烈酒 | 160 | medium-well 八分熟 | 143 |

# 習題解答

## Unit 2

### III

guests , luggage , storage , rent , pub , baggage , airport , thanked , enjoy

### IV

1.d  2.a  3.c  4.b  5.c

## Unit 3

### III

1.B  2.D  3.A  4.E  5.F  6.C

### IV

1.c  2.d  3.b  4.a  5.c  6.a

## Unit 4

### IV

1. I would like to change my room.
2. May I know your room and room number, sir?
3. Could you please spell your surname, ma'am?
4. I'm afraid all of our rooms are fully booked this evening.

### V

1.d  2.a  3.c  4.d

## Unit 5

### III

1.C  2.E  3.A  4.B  5.D

### IV

1.to,for/into  2.in/out,at, 3.the,in  4.the,on  5.for,in,a

## Unit 6

### IV

1.c  2.c  3.c  4.a  5.d

## Unit 8

### III

1.which  2.who  3.which 4.who  5.where  6.that / which  7.who  8.where

### IV

1. Would you like something to drink?

2. Are you ready to order?

3. How would you like your steak done?

4. Right now, we're having a special a pizza.

5. Our restaurant specializes in Sichuan and Cantonese food styles.

6. There's so much on your menu, it's hard to decide.

## Unit 9

### III

1. May I know your room number, so I can send someone?

2. We'll be there right away.

3. We need some more shampoo and soap.

4. I will send someone to your room right away.

5. For security reasons, I'm not allowed to open rooms for guests.

6. I'll contact maintenance for you, sir.

### IV

1.d  2.c  3.a  4.d  5.c

## Unit 10

### III

1. return  2. send  3. get

4. to be  5. offers  6. have

7. take  8. pick up , deliver

### IV

1. If you look in your dresser, you'll find laundry forms.

2. We'll send a babysitter to your room just before.

3. We'll try our best, ma'am, but we can't guarantee anything.

4. We have an express

laundry service at a 50 %
extra charge.

5. Can your laundry service
get out coffee stains.

## Unit 11

III

1. receive  2. cost  3. come

4. made    5. replaced

6. recommend

7. sending  8. take , pay

9. put      10. wrap

IV

1. May I weigh your letter,
please?

2. Is this stone a real emerald
or is this an imitation?

3. One has a rough surface
and one has a smooth
surface.

4. This tea is very popular
in China and well known

in other countries.

5. What kind of Chinese tea
do you recommend?

## Unit 12

III

1. D   2. A   3. H   4. F

5. B   6. G   7. E   8. C

IV

1. b   2. d   3. a   4.d

## Unit 13

III

1. made  2. buy  3. like

4. send   5. wrap  6. charged

7. carve  8. is    9. fill out

IV

1. That would be nice, but
we don't have Chinese
names.

2. In China, the dragon is a
symbol for men.

3. Those carpets are made

of wool and there are
many designs.

4. This is a large wool
carpet, so I suggest you
send it by sea.

5. We have all kind of little
animals carved from
marble.

**Unit 14**

IV

1. d    2. c    3. b

# 旅 館 英 語　　　　　　　　　餐 旅 叢 書

作　　　者／Andrew W. Peat

出 版 者／揚智文化事業股份有限公司

發 行 人／葉忠賢

執行編輯／陳冠霈

登 記 證／局版北市業字第1117號

地　　　址／台北市新生南路三段88號5樓之6

電　　　話／(02)2366-0309　2366-0313

傳　　　眞／(02)2366-0310

E - m a i l ／tn605547@ms6.tisnet.net.tw

網　　　址／http://www.ycrc.com.tw

郵政劃撥／14534976　揚智文化事業股份有限公司

印　　　刷／鼎易印刷事業股份有限公司

法律顧問／北辰著作權事務所　蕭雄淋律師

初版一刷／2000年8月

I S B N ／957-818-177-9

定　　　價／500元

國家圖書館出版品預行編目資料

Practical hotel English／Andrew W. Peat作.

-- 初版. -- 台北市 : 揚智文化 , 2000[民89]

面 ； 公分. -- （餐旅叢書）

內文爲英文, 中文題名 : 旅館英語

ISBN 957-818-177-9（平裝附光碟）

1. 英國語言 - 會話

805.188                          89010686